DOUBLE-CROSSED

DOUBLE-CROSSED

Ron Everhart

Copyright © 2024 by Ron Everhart.

Library of Congress Control Number: 2024911072
ISBN: Softcover 979-8-3694-2357-8
eBook 979-8-3694-2356-1

All rights reserved. No part of this book may be reproduced or transmitted in any form or by any means, electronic or mechanical, including photocopying, recording, or by any information storage and retrieval system, without permission in writing from the copyright owner.

This is a work of fiction. Names, characters, places and incidents either are the product of the author's imagination or are used fictitiously, and any resemblance to any actual persons, living or dead, events, or locales is entirely coincidental.

Any people depicted in stock imagery provided by Getty Images are models, and such images are being used for illustrative purposes only.
Certain stock imagery © Getty Images.

Print information available on the last page.

Rev. date: 11/08/2024

To order additional copies of this book, contact:
Xlibris
844-714-8691
www.Xlibris.com
Orders@Xlibris.com
859151

CONTENTS

Chapter 1 1
Chapter 2 8
Chapter 3 15
Chapter 4 22
Chapter 5 31
Chapter 6 36
Chapter 7 43
Chapter 8 51
Chapter 9 58
Chapter 10 64
Chapter 11 71
Chapter 12 77
Chapter 13 83
Chapter 14 91
Chapter 15 94
Chapter 16 99
Chapter 17 104
Chapter 18 111
Chapter 19 117
Chapter 20 124
Chapter 21 130

CHAPTER 1

*T*HE CLOUDS TO THE NORTH had the prospector worried. He was still a long way from his cabin and had a river to cross. Jeb Pearson was a middle-aged man who had left the city of San Francisco to join the number of increasing miners looking for gold. He had let his hair and beard grow long and stayed to himself, not allowing too many men or women close to him. Jeb liked people, but since the incident in San Francisco, he decided to forget everything and go his way.

Jeb was once a prominent lawyer. One night in a saloon, he had a run in with a saloon girl, he was seeing and she accused him of robbing and beating her. During a struggle with a gun, Melissa was shot and badly wounded.

Melissa said it was attempted murder, Jeb said it was self-defense. During the trial, his best friend, Joshua, helped him break out of jail. The two parted company and had not seen each other for ten years. Little did Jeb know that Joshua and Melissa had married and were looking for him in order to clear his name?

It still was not raining when Jeb came to the river. He urged his horse and mule into the river and crossed it with no problems. He made his way up the stream that flowed out of the mountains passed a small shack and barn built on the side of the mountain. He put the mule and horse in a make shift barn.

It would be winter in a few weeks and he needed to find enough gold to allow him to stay in town during the winter. The owners of the hotels and saloons would allow the miners to stay there for enormous amounts of money, which by spring often left the miners broke.

After putting the mule and horse in the barn, Jeb went down to the stream and began pounding on a large rock that was in the way of his new sluice chute. As he hit it with the sledgehammer a large piece of glittering rock, fell off it. He picked it up and examined it and it appeared to be solid gold. He did not get excited because, fool's gold had fooled him before. Jake put the rock in a sac and kept chipping the big rock.

Later in the day, he went back to the cabin. He fixed a meal and was eating, when he heard his name called. He picked up his rifle and walked over to the window. He looked out and saw the sheriff getting off his horse. Jeb walked over to the door and opened it. He stepped outside with his rifle held waist high aimed directly at the sheriff. The sheriff looked at Jeb with disdain, but raised his hands.

"What do you want?" Jeb asked puzzled by the sheriff's arrival.

"There's a fella in town that has been asking for the whereabouts of Jeb Pearson. Says he's been to every mining town around but can't find you. I know your names Jeb but I don't know your last name."

"What's this fella's name?" Jeb asked lowering his rifle.

"He never said."

Jeb rubbed his beard. "Keep them off this mountain. You know I don't like people snooping around."

"You know winters coming," the sheriff said as he looked to the north at the threatening clouds.

"Yeah, I know." Jeb said in a disgusted tone of voice. "That means I have to put up with people for about six months. You still rent me that little room behind the jail?"

"You know I will."

"Get on back to town and I'll be in, in a few days."

The sheriff mounted his horse and Jeb watched him until he was out of sight. The sheriff had proven to be a good friend.

Jeb went to bed and was sleeping soundly when the wind began blowing. The rain beat on the roof and side of the cabin awakening him. He got cold and covered himself with more blankets. After a while, the rain ceased and all was quiet.

The next morning Jeb got up and looked out the window. The creek was running out of its banks and had demolished most of his new sluice chute. He rubbed his head and walked back over to the bed. Nothing had gone right this summer. Every attempt at prospecting and finding gold had failed. He was nearly broke and needed for something positive to happen. He decided that as soon as the river went down he would go to town for the winter. He began packing the things he would need.

The next day the stream in front of the cabin was still flowing high. He went out to view the damage to his sluice chute and as he was looking down in the water when he saw several glittering rocks. He waded out into the stream and picked them up. Several of them were large and one was the size of his fist.

They were pure gold, but he could not let it out that he had found so much. He put the rocks into a bag and hid them in the shack. As he was preparing to move to town, he decided to take the smaller rocks with him and leave the bigger ones until he went back to California.

The next day he went to town and stopped at the Jail. The sheriff led him to the little room and gave Jeb the key.

"Have you seen any more of that fella looking for a fella named Jeb?"

"No," the sheriff said somberly. "I told him I did not know anyone by the name of Pearson. He was disappointed as was his lady friend. He told me they would be back before winter on their way south to Frisco."

"Humph," Jeb snarled. "He ain't looking for me. My friends ain't stupid enough to get married." Jeb looked at the sheriff who was frowning. "You're an exception; you got one of the few good women."

The sheriff chuckled. "I would like to know what has turned you against people so badly."

"Naw, you just think you do," Jeb said sadly.

Jeb rearranged the furniture in the room as he did every year. Mrs. Haymaker liked the room one-way, Jeb liked it another and he fixed it that way. After it was arranged the way he wanted, he lay down on the bed and began to wonder about things that had happened in the past.

A few days later, it began to snow and the nights were becoming longer. Jeb spent most of his time exercising trying to stay in shape for the coming summer of building new sluice chute.

One afternoon he slugged through the snow to the saloon. He was sitting at a table having a beer when the sheriff came in. When he saw Jeb, he joined him. "That fellas back in town, with his lady friend. They went as far north as they could go and never found you. He says he got good news if he can ever find you."

"Humph," Jeb grunted. "Sheriff, you're the only friend I got in this country. So I hope I can trust you never to tell anyone you know anyone by the name of Jeb."

"Pearson?" The sheriff asked.

"I never said that you did." Jeb said somberly.

"Jeb, I want to be your friend, but if you're running from the law, I have to detain you."

Jeb looked at the sheriff, "If I was running from the law and you tried to stop me, Mrs. Haymaker would be a widow. Aren't you glad I am not running from the law?" Jeb asked laughing. The sheriff forced a grin. Jeb got up and walked out of the saloon. Unknowingly, he passed the man who was looking for him.

The sheriff sat at the table thinking about what Jeb had said. A younger man wearing a suit joined the sheriff. His face was wrinkled and he looked tired. "Sheriff," the man said quietly. "The men tell me you house a man every winter by the name of Jeb."

"I told him and his name is not Pearson and he does not want to see you," the sheriff as he stood up. "He is trigger happy, so I would leave him alone."

"Tell him his name is cleared. Melissa dropped the charges and she and I are married. I am paying for it, but I married her."

The sheriff sat down. "Tell me what happened?"

"I thought you did not know him?"

"I don't, but since you're looking for him there has to be a story."

"Jeb was a prominent lawyer in Frisco. He was running around with a saloon girl named Melissa. They got into an argument and Melissa pulled a gun. In the struggle, Melissa was shot and charged Jeb with attempted murder. I broke him out of jail and we think he is here in Alaska looking for gold. In order to get the attempted murder charge against Jeb dropped, I agreed to marry Melissa. Now we are looking for him to give him the news."

"What about him breaking jail?"

"That's his fault."

The sheriff stood up. "I don't know any Jeb Pearson, sorry I can't help you."

The sheriff went to the room where Jeb was staying and knocked on the door. Jeb opened it. "Jeb," the sheriff said sadly. "I need to talk to you. It is important."

Jeb motioned the sheriff to come into the room and sit down. The man who is looking for you told me to tell you, your name has been cleared in the attempted murder case. In order to get your name cleared this fella married Melissa. You're still wanted for breaking jail."

Jeb nodded. "So the jail break was a set up. I wonder if Melissa was really shot. If I am in jail, there are people who can get to what is left of my money to build things in Frisco. Melissa and I got along good until I decided not to finance some projects. The next thing I knew I was up for attempted murder. Are you going to turn me in?"

"No. I am not," the sheriff said roughly. "From what I gather from you and this other fella is that you were framed. That does not go well in my book."

CHAPTER 2

During the winter, Jeb spent most of his time in his room. The sheriff knowing Jeb's desire to stay away from people often invited him to his house for dinner. Jeb always left a few gold chips off the rocks for the sheriff's wife to find. As a result, Mrs. Haymaker would only go to the store right after it opened or just before it closed. She always paid in gold chips and asked the clerk at the store to keep it quiet.

The winter turned cold with more snow than anyone could remember. It was difficult to get around unless an individual had snowshoes or a dog sled. Jeb soon had cabin fever and often went to the store with Mrs. Haymaker to help carry the groceries home. It was an extremely cold night when Jeb decided to go to the saloon. He sat at a table back in the corner where it was dark so he would not be noticed. A brunette whose face was covered with so much make up she looked artificial joined him. She reeked of a smelly perfume. She sat down beside him. Jeb did enjoy her low swooping neckline.

"Are you lonesome?" she purred.

"Not yet," he answered. "You're not getting me drunk so you're wasting your time. I came over here to get out of my room and that is all."

"I don't know your name," she whispered. "My husband was killed a month or so ago in a mining accident. The saloon owner offered me a job. I don't have to do anything with you as long as I get you to spend money on beer and whiskey. He told me the drunker they are the less I have to worry about things happening between us."

"Have you got a name?" Jeb asked

"Sharon."

"Who hired you to get me drunk?"

"Well my boss likes for me to get men drunk, so I will get paid whether anything happens or not. That man in the gray suit gave me fifty dollars to get you drunk and take you to my room."

Jeb nodded and looked hard at the man in the gray suit. "That man is one of the biggest crooks in Frisco! The worst thing you can do is trust him," Jeb said bitterly. "He was supposed to be my best friend. So go on your way."

Sharon looked into Jeb's eyes. "You're telling the truth, I can see it in your eyes."

"I'll give you a thousand dollars if you and I pretend I get drunk and I will go to your room with you. I would really like to talk to him."

Sharon swallowed hard. "A thousand dollars?" She whispered in amazement

"I'll give you a kiss besides."

"You don't need to give me a kiss, but a thousand dollars will get me back to California in the spring." Sharon said with excitement in her voice.

"There you go taking the fun out of working for me," Jeb said in a disgusted tone of voice.

"When do you want to do it?" She asked.

"Come spring," Jeb said happily. "In the meantime you can make a few bucks, do me a favor and bust up his marriage and be my girl!"

"What?" Sharon asked. "I don't want to break up any body's marriage. I certainly do not want to be your girl."

"I'll raise the ante to two thousand dollars. I will give you five hundred in advance. In the spring when we let him in your room, I'll pay you off."

Sharon's eyes got big. "You have got to be joking!"

Jeb pulled a wad of money out of his pocket. "Here's a hundred dollars to start you off. And no one is to know about this."

Sharon looked at Jeb, then the money and then at Jeb "You look like you can't even afford a beer."

"I want to keep it that way," Jeb said grinning. "I need to look as if I have been drinking when I go to your room."

"Wait a minute." Sharon left the table and walked over to Sandy. They talked for a few seconds and then Sharon rejoined Jeb.

Sandy brought two full bottles of whiskey and two empty bottles to the table. The empty bottles were slipped under the table while Sandy had her back to the main part of the saloon. A few minutes later one full bottle and an empty bottle of whiskey were on the table. Sharon slipped the second empty bottle on the table, she, and Jeb made their way to Sharon's room. Jeb purposely staggered and tripped twice so Sharon had to help him.

When they arrived at Sharon's room Jeb propped a chair under the door handle to keep anyone from opening it. He walked over to the bed and lay down on his back. "For what he's paying you, you think he would provide a better bed," Jeb said as he put his hands behind his head. "How about taking off that make up and joining me?"

"I am not a whore and do not want to be," Sharon said as she backed away from Jeb.

Jeb got up from the bed and walked over to her. He turned her around to face him. "I know you want to get back to California. I have the money and you know it. How much am I going to have to up the ante for you to sleep with me?"

"The only man I ever did it with was my husband."

Jeb put some money on the chest and walked back over to Sharon. She also saw him put some money back in his pocket. He took hold of her hand and led her to the wash pan. "I asked you to take off that make up so I could see what you really look like, but you won't, so I am going to do it." Jeb said as he put the washcloth in the water and wrung it out. He wiped Sharon's face several times and wrung out the washcloth before he was satisfied. He led her closer to the lamp. "You're a nice looking lady," he said as he turned her face so she was looking directly at the lamp. He took her by the hand and led her to the bed.

"But I don't want to," Sharon protested.

"You're not going to be," Jeb said as he sat down on the bed and as he lay down, he pulled Sharon by the arm until she was bent over as she struggled to keep from getting in the bed. "We both need some sleep. Take off my boots and let's get some sleep."

"You mean...."

"I am not leaving this bed. If you want to sleep in that chair that is fine. But it might get cold."

Sharon reluctantly took Jeb's boots off. "I am not your slave," she spat bitterly.

"You will do what I want because you want to go back to California."

"Everything but..."

"I understand that," Jeb said quietly. "Now come on."

Sharon looked at the money on the chest as she blew out the lamp. She sat down in the chair, but could not get comfortable. She looked at the darkened figure in her bed and decided to risk it. She got under the covers and tried to stay as far from Jeb as she could. Jeb remained on his back, put his arm under Sharon's shoulders and pulled her closer to him.

"No," she whispered.

"Lay on your side and put your head on my shoulder that is all I ask."

Sharon was perplexed at the behavior of this man. She had to fight off most men until they passed out. Finding herself comfortable, she laid her hand on his chest. It was not long until they were both asleep.

Joshua watched Sharon and Jeb go upstairs to her room. After a while, he began to wonder why Sharon did not come down stairs to get him. He walked over to the bartender. "My friend went up to a room upstairs and it's been a while. Can I go find him?"

"Which one of the girls did he go up with?"

"I don't know her name, but she was kinda pretty."

"If it was Sharon she's a prude, why anybody would want to spend the night with her is beyond me. She makes the boss a lot of money though. She keeps telling men how good it was and they don't remember. It takes a day or two for them to sober up." He said laughing. "No, you can't go up there. You don't want to go disturbing things do you? Besides I'm not telling you which room she is in."

"Where is Mr. Elliot?" Jeb asked

"He's retired for the night and I am getting ready to close," the bartender said giving Joshua the evil eye. "The way it's snowing out there, I'd better be getting home and so had you."

Joshua left the saloon and went to the hotel. He went to his room where Melissa was waiting.

"It took you long enough!" she spat hatefully.

"Yeah, I know, and I still didn't get to see him," Joshua said taking off his coat and throwing it on a chair. That saloon girl double-crossed me."

"You let a little hussy cheat you out of fifty dollars?" Melissa asked as she laughed.

"I suppose you could do it better?" Joshua asked sitting on the bed and taking his boots off.

"Jeb hates me and if he sees me he would probably kill me," Melissa said sadly. "I should have married him instead of accusing him of shooting me."

"It would nice of him to do me the favor," Joshua said lying down on the bed."

"But it won't happen, and you won't leave me, because I will go singing to the cops."

Joshua looked at Melissa with contempt. "To think I double-crossed my best friend for the likes of you."

Melissa walked over to him; she opened her dress so he could see most of her large breasts. "You like me and both of us know it," Melissa said as she lay beside him.

CHAPTER 3

*T*HE NEXT MORNING JEB WOKE with a start. He rose into a sitting position so fast he nearly jerked Sharon's head off.

"What is wrong?" she asked with fear in her voice.

Jeb lay back down and pulled Sharon close to him. "I was sleeping well, and then I had a bad dream."

"I haven't slept this good in a long time, Sharon whispered.

Jeb nodded. "It's been ten years or longer since I had a woman as close to me as you were last night." He kissed Sharon on the forehead. Jeb got out of bed, walked over to the chest and counted his money. "It seems you can be trusted too," Jeb said as he put his money in his pocket. He walked back over to the bed, took Sharon's hand and pulled her to her feet. "How about I buy you breakfast, instead of paying you cash."

"I have to have cash because Mr. Elliot gets a cut."

Jeb made a face. "He gets it both ways, money from the liquor and a cut from you girls."

"He calls it rent because we have a place to live," Sharon said sadly.

"I'll bet he charges you a high percent so he gets most of it, so you girls will always have to work for him."

Sharon nodded. "He gets onto me because I eat so much. I am trying to save my money."

"So you can go back to California?" Jeb asked frowning.

Sharon turned her back to Jeb. "I have family there, maybe I can start over."

"I have never heard such a sob story in my life. The problem is I believe you," Jeb sadly. "Elliot is taking advantage of you in ways that are no ways near right."

"Can I asked you to do something for me?" Sharon asked.

"I suppose," Jake said, smiling at Sharon.

"Shave your beard so I can see what you look like."

Jeb walked over to the window. Sharon followed him. "I can't Sharon; I am wanted by the law."

Sharon let out a little "Oh," as she covered her mouth.

"It is nothing serious," Jeb said as he looked at Sharon's pale face. "You don't need to be afraid of me. I was accused of attempted murder, during the trial I broke out of jail with the help of the man who hired you to get me drunk. I have been cleared of the attempted murder charge but I am wanted for breaking out of jail. Once I am back in jail, they think, things in Frisco can go on according to plan."

"A friend double-crossed you?" Sharon asked as she looked at Jeb with a puzzled look on her face.

Jeb nodded. "In a sense, last night we double-crossed him. I am sorry I used you," he said putting his hands on her shoulders. "I did not know what else to do." He pulled Sharon closer to him and to his surprise, she responded.

Sharon looked up into his eyes. "You're being honest with me and that's more than I can say for most of the men I have met up here."

Jeb took Sharon's hand and led over to the bed. He sat down and had her sit beside him. "Tell me about your husband's accident."

Sharon took a deep sigh and looked out the window. "He was dynamiting the base of a cliff. I heard a horrible noise. I went out on the porch and watched as the cliff buried my husband."

"How old are you?" Jeb ask he stroked his beard.

"Twenty. Why?" She asked with her voice full of questions.

Jeb plunged deep into thought as he looked at Sharon. "How much gold did your husband find?"

"Barely enough to keep us fed, Sharon said sadly as she looked out the window.

"After your husband's death, who approached you about working in the saloon?" Jeb asked turning Sharon to face him.

"A man, I see once in a while in the saloon. He is a miner, I guess. He is a big man with a red beard." Sharon said sadly, as she looked at Jeb. "Why all the questions?"

"I'm thinking like a lawyer, Jeb said as he looked at Sharon. "Does this miner ever talk to Mr. Elliot?"

"Not that I know of?" Sharon said as she looked out the window.

"This may be my last question and it may hurt," Jeb said as he put his arm around Sharon. "Have any of the other girls working here been bought in here by similar circumstances."

Sharon hesitated as she looked out the window. She turned to face Jeb. Sandy, her husband was killed during a robbery. She had enough money to get back to California, but was beaten and robbed. Now she drinks a lot. She spends most of the time in her room alone," Sharon said sadly. "I feel sorry for her."

"How long has she been here?" Jeb asked.

"Less than I have. What's wrong?" Sharon asked as fear entered voice.

"Nothing," Jeb said as he lied to her. He stroked his beard as he stood up and pulled Sharon to her feet. "Put on a dress that's not so wrinkled and we will go for breakfast."

"You don't like my dress?" she asked as she looked at it.

"I'd like it better if it was blue instead of red. But since you're in it does not matter what color it is?" Jeb walked over to her closet. He found a nice beige dress. He hung it on the dividing screen. "Wear this!"

"The sleeves are long and it comes up to my neck and down to my feet, Sharon protested as she walked behind the screen. "I'm a saloon girl remember?"

"Yeah, I remember," Jeb, said peaking over the screen. "You're a saloon girl that does not want to be a saloon girl."

Sharon went behind the screen to change into the dress Jeb wanted her to wear "Will you quit looking over this screen? I know you like what you're looking at, but ...," Sharon said pretending to be angry as she fixed her hair.

"You're the only one who said, I liked looking at you," Jeb said as he grinned and looked over the screen.

"If that's the case, why are you taking me to breakfast?"

"Because you said you would go with me," Jeb said in a near whisper.

"And that's the only reason? Sharon asked with disappointment in her voice.

"It's as good of a reason as I can think of," Jeb said as he sat down on the bed. "I wish you would hurry, I'm hungry."

Sharon stepped from behind the screen. "Do I look presentable?" Jeb looked at her with astonished eyes. She was adorable in the beige dress with her brown hair hanging down to her waist.

"Did the man that suggested you come to work here ever visit your mine?"

"Not that I know of, why?"

Jeb shook his head. "Just wondering."

"You're thinking something what is it?" Sharon asked as she was getting upset at Jeb.

"I am hungry aren't you?"

"You're changing the subject!" Sharon spat hatefully.

"Yes, madam, I am, and trust me it will best if I tell you later."

Sharon put her hand in the crook of Jeb's elbow as they walked down the stairway to the entrance of the saloon. Mr. Elliot was sitting at a table doing some paper work when he saw them coming down the stairs. He stood up and greeted them.

Jeb looked at this man dressed in a dark blue suit, with his hair slicked back and his graying mustache dyed black.

"Good morning Sharon, Mr. Elliot said happily. "You look rested. It must have been a good night!"

"It was," Sharon said coldly. "This man is absolutely wonderful."

"That's the first time I have ever heard you comment on how good a man was." The grin on Mr. Elliot's face made Jeb sick.

"What will it cost me if I am her only customer?"

"You can't afford her!" Mr. Elliot said laughing at Jeb.

"You never answered my question." Jeb said with anger.

"A hundred dollars till you go back to the mine, and then she goes back to her regular work." Mr. Elliot said.

"I'll give you fifty dollars." Jeb said smiling.

"Sorry, for her to be yours alone will cost you a hundred dollars not a penny less, plus taking care of her meals." Mr. Elliot said.

A look of fear crossed Sharon s face.

"I'll discuss it with her and I'll get back with you," Jeb said almost pulling Sharon out the door. When they were out of earshot of the saloon Jeb turned to Sharon. "I know it was not the fifty dollars that scared you; I think your worth more than that. I wanted to see how bad he wanted to keep you as a regular girl. What frightened you?"

Sharon smiled weakly. "The fact, he thinks I'm worth a hundred dollars and you think I am worth fifty.

"I would have gone up to two hundred, but no higher."

"What am I to you?" She asked as anger filled her voice.

"A lady in trouble. Now what frightened you?

"The man that came in the door while we were talking to Mr. Elliot was the one that suggested I go to work in the saloon." He said, 'Mr. Elliot paid good but he doesn't.'"

When I told Mr. Elliot, "no," he asked me who would hire me if they knew I really wanted to be a saloon girl. "All Mr. Elliot wants is women to make him money."

Jeb stopped and looked back toward the saloon. "In a sense you were double-crossed. You know if the girls are already here he does not have to pay to bring them here."

Sharon stopped walking. "You mean my husband was murdered, so I could become a sex slave?"

"What about Sandy's husband?"

"I'm not hungry," Sharon said as her voice trembled. "I cannot believe what you just told me."

"I could be wrong!" Jeb emphasized.

The couple entered the crowded restaurant and found a table. Jeb helped Sharon with her chair and sat across from her. "This is not the time to talk about this. Enjoy your breakfast."

As they were eating, Jeb watched Sharon. "You know for you not to be hungry you sure are eating a lot."

Mr. Elliot feeds us one meal a day. "I am saving my money so that's all I eat. Since your buying, I am going to eat well."

"I used you last night, so you're using me today?"

Sharon nodded. "I think it's a fair trade."

CHAPTER 4

Jeb gave Mr. Elliot one hundred dollars so he would be Sharon's only customer. Mr. Elliot decided when Jeb was not at the saloon; Sharon had to work the tables to help get the men drunk. As Mr. Elliot soon discovered it was a decision that would cost him money. Saturday night the sheriff invited Jeb to eat dinner at his house. Jeb accepted the invitation, but did not tell the sheriff what he suspected about Mr. Elliot. It was late when Jeb walked into the saloon. He looked the crowd over and saw Sharon sitting at a table with three men. One was always reaching over and trying to pull the strap of Sharon's dress off her shoulder. Jeb hurried over to the table. As the man reached for her strap again, Jeb took out his revolver and hit the man's hand with it. The man screamed in pain as he grabbed his hand.

The saloon became quiet and all eyes were on the table where Jeb was standing.

"What is the matter with you?" A short fat man asked. "He was just having a little fun."

"You're not having that kind of fun with my girl," Jeb said as he put his gun back in its holster.

A tall, lanky man stood up. He handed the fat man his hat. "She ain't your girl she's ours. We were getting ready to pay her when you interfered."

"But you had not asked the lady had you?" Jeb asked staring coldly at the man.

"You don't gotta ask, all you gotta do is have the money." A tall skinny miner yelled.

Jeb stood his ground. "With this lady there is no asking. She is mine, bought and paid for. Besides that she does not want to be with any of you fella's except to get you drunk so Mr. Elliot can become a rich man."

"Are you telling me I can't spend any more nights with this woman?"

"That's almost correct. Except it's, you cannot spend any more nights with this lady," Jeb said, as he walked over to Sharon.

"She's not a lady, she's a saloon girl and I will spend the night with her if I want too.

"Try it," Jeb said as he took Sharon's hand and she stood up. The tall, skinny man looked at Sharon's sly grin. He swallowed hard. He reached out to hold Sharon's hand.

"Come on Sharon, I'll pay you twice what he's paying you."

Sharon jerked her hand free of the miner s hand. "I am not going with you. This man is my only customer. I am bought and paid for. He is the only man allowed in my room," she said as she put her arm around Jeb.

If there's a fight watch Elliot," Jeb whispered.

The miner grabbed for Sharon, but missed. He doubled up his fist and walked around the table. Sharon hurried to the opposite side of the table and picked up a whiskey bottle by the neck. She waited as she held it behind her back. The miner swung at Jeb and missed. Jeb hit the miner square in the jaw. The miner staggered and fell to the floor. The fat man put his arms around Jeb from behind. The skinny miner got up from the floor and hit Jeb in the face. Sharon ran behind the fat miner and hit him over the head with the bottle, sending glass everywhere and the miner to the floor. The skinny miner looked at Sharon who was still holding the remains of the bottle. He lunged for and grabbed her around the waist and both of them fell to the floor. The miner was preparing to hit Sharon when Jeb grabbed his arm and began twisting it. As the miner got up Sharon, pushed her dress back down as far as it would go as she stood up. Jeb hit the miner sending him falling across a table. The table tipped sending him to the floor. The men in the saloon began whooping it up, some were for the miner and some were for Jeb. As he got up the miner picked up a chair and swung it over his head at Jeb. Jeb moved and the chair broke as it smashed the table. Jeb clipped the miner on the chin, knocking him down. Jeb pulled the miner to his feet and hit him in the face again, then hit him in the stomach and planted a fist in his face that rendered him unconscious.

Jeb stretched out his hand toward Sharon. She took his hand in hers and they started up the stairway. The fat man drew his revolver and aimed it at Jeb. Jeb drew his revolver and pushed Sharon behind him. He shot at the man's feet. The man danced a little jig to keep his feet from being hit by the bullets.

"I could have killed you fat man, but I didn't. Next time you draw on me I will," Jeb yelled, pushing Sharon up the stairs so she would get the idea, he was in a hurry. When they arrived in her room, Sharon sat on the bed and Jeb sat down beside her.

"Thanks for hitting the fat man with the bottle. He had a good grip and it was difficult to break." Jeb lay backwards until he was lying on his back. He took hold of Sharon's arm and tugged on it. Sharon lay down then rolled on to her side. She positioned herself so her head was on Jeb's shoulder. She placed her hand on his chest. A few minutes later, there was a knock on the door.

Jeb put his hand over Sharon's mouth. "Get behind the screen and put on the beige dress. Hurry."

Sharon quickly got behind the screen and as soon as her dress was hanging over the top of the screen, Jeb opened the door. He was not surprised to see the sheriff.

"Well Jeb, what do you say for yourself?" The Sheriff asked.

"Self-defense. I paid Mr. Elliot one hundred dollars so I could be Sharon's only customer and to top that off I have to feed her."

"Jeb," the sheriff said as he took a sigh. "Where did you get a hundred dollars?"

"I saw him pay Mr. Elliot," Sharon said from behind the screen.

"Look lady, you're a saloon girl and we all know you take up for the men your with."

Sharon came from behind the screen wearing the beige dress. "But I was not with anyone until Jeb and I started up the stairway."

The sheriff looked at the lady from top to bottom and back again. "Mrs. Johnson! What are you doing here?"

Jeb shut the door.

"I couldn't find a job and…..." Sharon said slowly.

"So you became a whore?"

"No," Sharon sobbed. "I have never done it with anyone but my husband. I get men so drunk they pass out and do not remember anything. Then I brag on them and they think they don't remember."

"That's awfully close to stealing."

"What happened downstairs that brought you over here?" Jeb asked loudly.

"The skinny miner was so mad he threw three bottles into the supply of whiskey behind the bar. It did a lot of damage. Mr. Elliot may not have enough liquor to last the winter."

"Well sheriff," Jeb said quietly. "It's all her fault. She was flirting with them, like she does all the men. She made that fat fella mad when she hit him in the head with a whiskey bottle for no reason at all. I mean she clobbered him good. I think a couple of days in jail would do her good."

"Jeb, how can you, I was trying to protect you."

"Better handcuff her too; I suspect she can be a wild one." Jeb said as he winked at Sharon. "Where do you keep your money?

You and I both know they are going to look for it so you will be broke and have to stay here."

"Some is in the bottom drawer of the chest, some is in the closet and some is under the mattress," Sharon said as anger filled her voice.

"You're smart not keeping all your money together," he said as he stuffed her money into his pockets.

"Jeb, I don't understand." Sharon said with confusion in her voice.

"I thought you wanted out of here?"

"I do."

"Is that what is happening?" Jeb asked.

Sharon smiled. "For a day or two."

The sheriff handcuffed Sharon's hands behind her back. He took Jeb's revolver out of its holster and pointed it at him. "Let's go," he said.

Sharon, Jeb and the sheriff walked down the stairway. The sheriff waved to the skinny miner with Jeb's revolver motioning him to join the parade. He walked over to Jeb and cursed him. The four of them walked to the jail. The miner was put in the cell the farthest from the office, which Jeb thought was strange. Sharon was put in the cell nearest the office, which made Jeb do some thinking. Jeb and the sheriff went to the office. Jeb told him what he thought about Sharon and Sandy working in the saloon. The sheriff agreed the circumstances under which both men died were highly unusual. Later that evening the sheriff went home.

Jeb went through his official files. Sharon's husband died in a mining accident. Sandy's husband disappeared, evidently killed in a mining accident and was buried by the debris. Sandy was robbed when she was preparing to board the boat to Washington. There was no mention of a beating. Jeb put the files back in the same order they were in and made it look as if they had not been bothered.

He went back into the cellblock. The miner was snoring in his sleep. Jeb opened Sharon's cell door as quietly as possible. He walked over to her and knelt beside the bunk. He put his hand over her mouth and awakened her. He motioned her to follow him as he led her to his room. He lit the lamp and as soon as Sharon saw the bed, she laid down. Jeb lay beside her. "Wake up Sharon. This is no time to sleep." Sharon insisted on sleeping. Jeb rolled her over on her back, put his arms around her and kissed her. Sharon realizing what was happening awakened quickly. She struggled until she realized it was Jeb. She pushed him away from her. Jeb quickly covered her mouth with his hand. "It was the only way I could wake you up. Listen to me." Sharon nodded. "I may have put our lives in danger."

The sheriff's official records tell me what we talked about you and Sandy being true and the sheriff's in on it. Whether you like it or not you have to go back to that saloon until spring. That's only about two months away. Can you ride a horse? Sharon shook her head 'No.' I can guarantee your life would not be worth anything on the boat going to California."

"What am I going to do?" she asked clinging to Jeb.

"Go with me to the mine."

Sharon looked at him with disgust. "I am beginning to think you are making this up so you can take me to the mine to be your whore."

Jeb stood up. "Believe what you want," he said reaching for her hand grasping it and pulling her to her feet. "In the meantime, it's back to your cell." As he locked Sharon's cell he looked at her darkened figure. "If I was you I would be quiet about what you and I have talked about. I hope you realize I am the only one you can trust."

Sharon sat down on her bunk and tried to think. It was not long until she fell into a troubled sleep. The next morning she woke early. She looked down the cellblock to see the skinny miner hanging against the bars. She screamed as loudly as possible. Jeb came running out of his room into the cellblock. Sharon pointed toward the miner's cell.

Jeb walked toward the cell. The cell door was locked. Jeb quickly put two and two together. He ran and got the keys to Sharon's cell. As he unlocked the cell door, he looked sadly at Sharon. "Do you want to believe, I did it? The miner, you, the sheriff are the only ones the murders were discussed with. The miner never heard anything, but was probably, eliminated to scare you and frame me."

"Where do you get all these crazy ideas?"

"I am a lawyer and was double-crossed twice. It looks as if you and I both are being double-crossed. Only I played into their hands thinking I could trust the sheriff."

"This is the only dress I have."

"Oh gees, what a time to worry about clothes! Jeb said in aggravation as he walked away from her cell. "Are you coming or staying?"

Sharon looked at the miner s body hanging against the bars. "I'm coming."

CHAPTER 5

The cold wind hit Jeb and Sharon as they left the jail. Jeb took Sharon to the stable and hid her under the hay where she would be relatively warm. He made his way to the back of the saloon and found the back door unlocked. The saloon was dark and he did not know what to expect. He waited until his eyes adjusted better to the dark before he started up the stairway. He slipped into Sharon's room and lit the lamp. He covered the light with his hand, so it would not be obvious from the outside someone was in Sharon's room.

He opened her closet, found her winter coat, boots and grabbed a few of her dresses. He closed the closet door and made his way down the stairway and out the back door. He felt the barrel of a gun in his back.

The sheriff thought you might try to run after killing the miner, so let's go back to the jail.

Jeb turned to face the man. You can't mean the sheriff hung him to frame me and scare Sharon into staying.

"Better than that, you two are going to be shot while trying to escape."

"I see," Jeb said as he suddenly pushed the clothes upward against the man's revolver causing it to fire. Jeb dropped the clothes and smashed the man in the face. The man slipped on some ice and fell to the ground. As he was getting up Jeb, hit him in the head with his revolver. Jeb picked up the clothes and ran. He stayed behind the buildings until he was near the stable. He ran inside and crawled under the hay with Sharon.

It was not long until several men were in the stable. His horse and mule are still here, they are hiding somewhere in town, the sheriff yelled. If they get away, all of us will go to jail.

A few minutes later, all was silent. "We have to stay here," Jeb whispered.

"I'm glad I came with you," Sharon whispered as she moved hay until she was lying on her back. I didn't know what to do, your kindness won out.

Jeb lay on his stomach beside her. He folded his arms and laid his head on them. "I think we will go to the mine. We will be safe until someone sees the smoke from the fire."

Sharon extended her arms toward Jeb. She put one of them around his head and pulled him toward her. "You owe me a kiss," she whispered. Jeb kissed her passionately. Sharon held him as tight as she could.

"Whew!" She whispered when they finished. She lay with her eyes closed. "I have never been kissed like that before!"

"Wait until this beard is shaved off."

"I don't think, I could stand it," she whispered.

"You're just all excited about getting away from that bunch of crooks," Jeb whispered as he kissed her again…gently.

"I never said you could kiss me again."

"Yeah, I know, but I figure what the heck. You can't yell at me without giving our location away. I know you don't want to be murdered or go back to jail. So what, if I kiss you." Jeb promptly kissed her again. To his surprise, she responded. "Why didn't you object?"

"If you are going to kiss me anyway, I might as well enjoy it too. When all this is over what will happen to us, will one or both of us be dead or what?"

"I wish I could tell you," Jeb whispered as he kissed her again. "We might as well enjoy one another as much as you will let us," he whispered kissing her again. Suddenly he raised his head and covered her mouth with his hand. "Shhh, someone is coming."

"His horse and mule are still here," the sheriff said. "Jake you stay here and guard the place. Kill him, do whatever you want to with her. Make sure they are both dead."

Sharon put her arms around Jeb and held him tight. "I'm scared." She whispered.

"So am I," Jeb whispered back. He kissed her passionately. Sharon responded and held him tightly and running her hand though his hair and rubbing his back.

"Take it easy," he whispered as he rubbed her back. "There's a guard down there that would like to shoot us," Jeb said as he kissed her on the neck and ears.

Suddenly, Jeb covered Sharon's nose and mouth with his hand smothering her. "We have to stop," he whispered. "I don't want to either, but we have to or give ourselves away." Sharon nodded her head in agreement.

They lay in silence looking at one another. Sharon was wondering if it was love, lust or safety that was allowing her to let Jeb do what he did. Jeb looked at Sharon and grinned. She was a good-looking woman, definitely well built and desirable was not quite the word to describe her.

"Hey Jake."

"Hey Tom."

"Any sign of them?"

"It's been quite. Any news?"

"Yeah, there's a man and a woman from California that's looking for old Jeb. Jeb tried to kill her and he broke out of jail. There's a reward for him dead or alive."

"What about this lady, I mean she seemed kinda nice. I was with her two nights and she told me for being as inexperienced as I was, we had a great time. She was right I drank too much and don't remember."

"Well the boss told me if I found her to do whatever I wanted then kill her. There's a thousand dollar reward for her body."

Sharon closed her eyes and leaned back so her neck was exposed to Jeb face. He looked at her face, her neck and let his eyes drift to her breast. He shook his head. 'How could I be so lucky,' he thought.

Jeb kept watching the light of day beneath the door of the stable. The light turned dark and Jeb figured it was dark outside. He put his finger over her lips telling Sharon to be quiet. He crept out from under the hay and made his way to where he could see the guard. The guard heard the rustling in the hay and climbed up to the hay mound. Jeb slammed him in the head with his revolver. The guard fell to the floor and never moved. Jeb climbed down from the loft, lit a lantern, knelt down beside the guard and began tying him up.

As Sharon climbed down the ladder, Jeb looked up at her. 'It sure would be nice if it was day light!' he thought to himself.

Jeb quickly saddled two horses. "Can you ride?"

"I have to, whether I can or not." Jeb helped her into the saddle, threw his saddlebags on the mule and mounted his horse. They went out the back way and made their way to the sheriff's house. He left Sharon on her horse while he went to the house. He pounded on the back door until the sheriff opened it. Jeb jammed his revolver into the sheriff's face. You and the misses get in here and lay on the floor. When the couple was laying on the floor Jeb motioned Sharon to come in the house.

"Get all the food that can be kept and put it in the saddle bags while I tie this lovely couple up." Sharon did as she was told. Jeb tied the sheriff's feet and legs together from behind him. He began tying up the sheriff's wife. "I want you to explain to her why this is happening and how you and the gang go about killing husbands to get their young wives to work as saloon girls. I really wonder if your cut is worth it."

CHAPTER 6

Jeb and Sharon rode out of town, across a wide valley. The sun was coming up as they passed a lake surrounded by majestic snow covered mountains. The river was high, as the snowmelt had begun. It was crossed with no problems except for Sharon being scared.

They traveled up the stream to where Jeb's cabin was located. He dismounted as did Sharon and he led the horses into the barn. He helped Sharon carry the supplies into the cabin.

"It ain't as bad as it looks," Jeb said, as he walked to the door and opened it for her.

Sharon walked inside and looked around her. The cabin was well built, but the furniture was covered with dust and the windows were dirty. "You lived here?" She asked in disbelief.

"Yeah, it ain't so bad in the summer, Jeb said as he put the saddlebags on the table.

"It's not what you're used to being fancy and all. It's a miner's cabin, used three maybe four months out of the year.

Sharon brushed off a chair and sat down. "Maybe I can fix it up a bit."

"You won't have time. We're leaving in the morning." Jeb said.

"Where are we going?" She asked.

"Over that mountain!" Jeb said pointing to the south.

"That tall one?" Sharon asked with apprehension.

Jeb chuckled. "I know it looks bad, but there's a pass that can't be seen from here. A friend of mine has a cabin over there. I go in Fairbanks for supplies and he goes into Wasatch."

"How long will it take for the Sheriff to get here?" She asked.

"We ought to leave in an hour or so," Jeb said as he pulled Sharon close to him. "When we do, both of us will be wrapped in four blankets plus our winter clothing. It is going to be cold! Right now we need to be sleeping."

Sharon turned away from him and walked over to the window. "If I had known it was going to be like this I would have never let you be my only customer."

Jeb put his hands on her shoulders and turned her to face him. "They would have worn you down eventually, or you would be like Sandy and drink too much. Mr. Elliot would own you. You're a free woman," he said extending his arms outward.

Sharon nodded. "Yes and the word free is in the word freezing."

"I like your sense of humor," he said chuckling. He turned serious.

"I am wanted by the law for a crime I did not commit. You are wanted so they can kill you and keep your mouth shut. Would you rather stay here and have them kill you or die trying to be a free woman?" Jeb ask.

"You have such a way with words," Sharon said as she walked over to the bed and sat down.

"Lay down and I'll cover you up." He said.

"Aren't you going to sleep?" She ask.

Jeb nodded. "I figure right now you don't want me near you. So I'll wait until you're asleep."

Sharon looked at him sadly. "Come," she whispered.

Jeb lay down beside her. "I have a new pair of boots you can wear when we cross the mountain."

"Go to sleep," she whispered as she lay her head on his shoulder.

Sharon was soon asleep. Jeb got up and went down to the creek and began panning for gold. He had to have money to keep him and Sharon alive.

It was morning when Mr. Elliot entered the stable. He was surprised to find the guard tied and gagged. "How did they get the best of you?" he yelled bitterly.

"They were in the hayloft."

"It figures," Mr. Elliott said hatefully.

Mr. Elliott hurried to the sheriff's office to tell him what had happened. When the sheriff was not in his office, Mr. Elliot went to the sheriff's house. When he found the sheriff and his wife tied up, he was angry. He took his cigar out of his mouth. "The boss ain't gonna like this."

Mr. Elliot hurried back to the saloon. He walked over to one of his men and they turned their backs to the main part of the saloon so they could not be heard. "Round up as many men as you can. You know, he is headed for his cabin. Tell the miners he killed the ole skinny miner and Sharon helped him. If it will help tell them every one who rides with you until they are caught gets free whiskey and girls for the night."

Sandy, a petite little brunette, was cleaning glasses behind the bar and heard what Mr. Elliot had said. When the sheriff and Mr. Elliot left the saloon, she took a bottle of whiskey and went to her room. She looked at herself in the mirror wondering what had happened to the young lady who once was happy, but was now a drunk. She huddled up in a chair and drank until she passed out and fell to the floor.

Joshua rushed into his room at the hotel. "A posse is going after Jeb and the girl. He hung a miner at the jail. I gotta go to make sure they don't kill him."

"Jeb hung a man?" Melissa asked in disbelief.

"That's what the sheriff said."

"I don't believe it, Jeb's to honest for that," Melissa said as she lit a cigarette.

"This miner and Jeb got in a fight over this saloon girl. They were in jail and Jeb hung him."

"That ain't right," Melissa argued. "If they were in separate cells how did Jeb hang him?"

Joshua looked at Melissa. "Maybe they were in the same cell. I don't know."

"They don't keep prisoners in the same cell. I know I been in jail enough times to know."

Joshua looked at Melissa strangely. "I don't understand you. You accuse Jeb of shooting you when the bullet missed; talk me into helping him break out of jail, black mail me into marrying you and now your defending Jeb. What is wrong with you, besides being crazy?"

"Aren't you going to kiss me goodbye?"

"No!" Joshua yelled as he walked out the door and slammed it.

Melissa walked over to the chest and poured herself a glass of brandy. "I hope Jeb shoots you, and then I will be a rich widow."

Jeb woke up to find Sharon gone. He got out of bed and lit the lamp. She was not in the cabin. He went to the barn to find the horses and mule was still there. He saw the silhouette of an individual walking toward the cabin from the creek. He walked toward the individual. "What are you doing out here?" he asked.

"Thinking," she said sadly. "I don't know if I have gotten you into trouble or you have gotten me into trouble. I'm trying to figure out what has happened these last few hours.

A lot has happened. I never suspected when we met that we would be standing in the middle of Alaska in the middle of the night talking about the trouble we are in. Really, Sharon we ought to be on the trail. It's going to be cold. But I would rather freeze to death a free man than hang for a crime I did not commit."

Sharon nodded. "If you had not come along, I don't know what would have happened to me." She looked into Jeb's eyes. "I still don't know and it scares me."

"That makes two of us," Jeb said taking her hand. "But I got an idea."

"Wonderful," Sharon said with as much enthusiasm as a corpse.

'What we'll do is go on the other side of that ridge. That will put us a good two hours ahead of them. If they turn back we can wait till they go back and go over the mountain."

"Jeb," Sharon said impatiently. "When are they going to get here? It's nighttime, it's winter! Instead of turning back, they are going to sleep. So we might as well go on over the mountain."

"It's going to be cold," Jeb warned.

Jeb went into the cabin, packed the supplies and tied them securely to the mule. He saddled the horses and went back into the cabin.

"I had to put on three pairs of socks before the boots would fit," Sharon said happily. "These are nice boots."

"Good. You can have them. How's the water?" Jeb ask.

"It's starting boil," she said as she walked over to the stove.

"We have four canteens. Keep them as close to your body as you can. They will help keep you warm. As they cool off put them closer to your heart. The blood will be warm as it goes through your body thus keeping you warm."

Sharon put her arms around Jeb neck and kissed him. "I am beginning to like you," she whispered. "If it were not for the trouble we are in we could ………."

"I know," Jeb cut in, "the trouble always interferes." He held Sharon close to him. "As soon as the canteens are hot we need to go."

Sharon turned away from him and walked back to the stove. "Are you going to help me with the canteens?" Jeb walked up behind her and put his arms around her waist. He kissed the back of her neck. "Jeb, please you tell me we need to go and then you start kissing me."

"I like you too, from the first night I was with you."

CHAPTER 7

*T*HE POSSE LEFT TOWN AT a full gallop. It was not long until the horses were tired from running in the melting snow. The sheriff had the posse slowed the horses to a walk.

Joshua rode up to be beside the sheriff. "If we don't hurry they are going to get away."

"Have you ever been to his cabin?"

"No,"

"It's in a huge box canyon surrounded by mountains. There ain't no way they can get out except go over a pass. It would take a fool to even think about trying to get over that mountain."

The posse eventually reached the cabin, which was abandoned.

"They didn't leave us no food and we didn't bring any," one of the men yelled as he stepped back out on the porch.

"There's tracks going up stream toward that mountain," another man yelled.

The sheriff looked at the mountain. "They'll be stubborn enough to make it," he sheriff said to himself.

Joshua walked over to the sheriff. "Is that the mountain you spoke of?"

"Yes," the sheriff said as he started to mount his horse. "The snow melt is on and the chances of them making it to Wasatch are slim to none. Burn the cabin. That way they don't have anything to come back to."

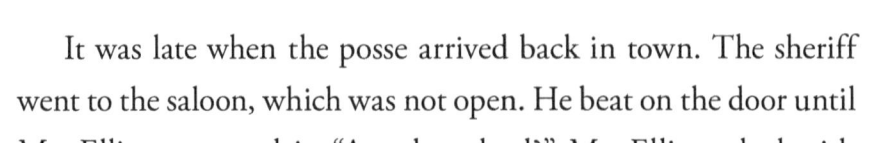

It was late when the posse arrived back in town. The sheriff went to the saloon, which was not open. He beat on the door until Mr. Elliot answered it. "Are they dead?" Mr. Elliot asked with desperation in his voice.

"They just as well be," the sheriff said as he pushed past Mr. Elliot and walked to the bar. "I'm cold, hungry and thirsty." Mr. Elliot walked behind the bar and poured the sheriff a shot of whiskey. "What do you mean they just as well be?"

"We burned the cabin so they have no place to go. They started for the pass that is south of his cabin. The railroad thought about that a few years ago. There are a lot of landslides and the wind rushes right through that pass from the north. They haven't got a chance."

"I hope your right," Mr. Elliot said with anger in his voice. "That man has lived up there ten years and probably knows every crook and cranny in those mountains. I hope your right, but something tells me you're wrong."

Joshua opened the door to his hotel room to find Melissa sleeping soundly. He lit a lamp, walked over to the bed and sat down on the edge of it. He began shaking Melissa's shoulder.

"Leave me alone," she moaned. "You had some last night."

Joshua grabbed Melissa by the hair and jerked her head backwards.

"Who had some last night because it wasn't me?"

Melissa put her hand at the back of her neck. "You're hurting me!"

"Who are you talking about?" Joshua yelled. "I want to know who?"

"I was dreaming," she said her voice racked with pain. "You know you are the only one I love and will let touch me."

"Right," Joshua said loudly as he flung Melissa's head down on the pillow.

Melissa sat up. "Did you find them?"

"No!" he said bitterly. "The tracks indicated they headed over a pass that the sheriff claims they will be killed because of the landslides and cold weather. They probably followed us back to town."

The couple climbed higher up the pass. Sharon looked behind them. "Do I see a faint column of smoke?"

Jeb looked back. "They burned the cabin," he said sadly.

"Now where we will live?" Sharon asked in despair.

"If we survive this pass, we'll build a nicer one."

"What with our good looks?"

"With your looks we could build a mansion. With my looks, we'd be lucky to have a shack. There's gold in that creek. No one knows it but me and you."

The couple proceeded up the pass. Jeb pointed to a rock ledge that would shelter them from the wind. They dismounted and huddled close to one another for body heat.

When the clouds began to cover the moon and build into the sky the couple started up the pass. The last part of the north side was extremely steep and the horses had a difficult time maneuvering through the snow. At last, the top was reached and the couple stopped. "Tell me where you have seen anything more beautiful," Jeb said as he looked around him. "I like coming up here in the summer. Can't stay to long because of the cold."

"Does it ever get warm up here?" Sharon asked as she admired the lofty snow covered mountains that surrounded her.

"Naw, it stays cold in the summer and freezing in the winter. But what a place to live!"

"How do we get down from here? That way looks awful steep." Sharon said as she looked down the south side of the pass.

"Is it going to be more difficult than what we came up?" she asked with fear in her voice.

"The easy part is over," Jeb said smiling. "When the railroad looked at this they decided the pass was impossible and they told everyone that. Everyone believed them. There were more landslides that year than old Tom can remember. He lives at the bottom of the pass. We visit one another and help one another. We are the only two that work these mountains. When he decides to go home to Colorado, he is going to be a rich man if he keeps his mouth shut. It's one of the secrets to surviving up here."

"So I have gathered," Sharon said. "If I hadn't told you my problems, I would not be in this mess."

"That's true," Jeb said looking at Sharon with lustful eyes even though she was bundled in coats and blankets. "You'd be a whore sooner or later or a dead one when the boys caught on to how you were stealing from them. You're a desirable woman, even if I can't see you. I know what I got and you are not getting away from me."

"You are confusing me."

Jeb rested his arms on the horn of his saddle and looked at Sharon. "There's nothing confusing to it. The first night we were together, you laid your cards on the table. At that time, you were not going to change your values. Despite the things that have happened between us, you still haven't. A horse is a good thing to have, but so is a good woman."

Sharon smiled as a tear fell from her eye. Jeb had taken the long way around to tell her he admired her, but stopped short of saying he loved her or did he? 'At least I am as valuable as a good horse.' She thought to herself.

"Follow me," he said smiling at her. She returned his smile.

Jeb dismounted, as did Sharon. She was surprised to find she was walking on a thin layer of snow, which covered the rocks. The couple followed the base of a cliff as it went down the mountainside. She saw a large arrow painted on the side of the cliff. Jeb turned to the right and started down a steep embankment. She was again surprised the snow was not deep. They entered a spruce forest of twisted trees and came to the side of a frozen lake.

Jeb looked over to Sharon. "It's pretty isn't? Look how far we came down."

Sharon stood amazed at the distance they had traveled. She smiled happily. "Are we going to make it?"

"It depends on the snow."

The couple went around the lake to where another arrow was painted on the cliff. Sharon marveled at the site of a frozen waterfall as they passed it on their way down the steep incline. The cold wind kept her from looking at the falls to long. Once again, they entered a spruce forest. Jeb stopped walking and stopped at looked back at the waterfall.

"I have never seen anything so beautiful," she said happily, as she put her arm around Jeb.

Jeb put his arm around Sharon. "The only thing more beautiful is you and you're still alive."

Sharon laid her head on Jeb chest. "It seems we have broken every rule in the book. Can I break another one?"

"No one will know it but you and I."

Sharon looked up into Jeb's eyes. "Women are not supposed to say this, but Jeb I am growing in love with you."

"Hell, woman, I been in love with you since the first night we were together. Why do you think I paid for you?"

Sharon laid her head on Jeb's chest. "I never thought I would ever hear a man tell me he loved me again."

Jeb put his finger under her chin and tilted her head until he could see her face. They kissed gently.

"Oh Jeb, you are my hero."

Jeb smiled. "Whatever that word is for a lady hero, that's what you are to me."

The couple walked through the forest until they came to another lake. It was frozen over and the snowdrifts around it looked deep. There was a distance of fifteen feet between a cliff and the shore of the lake.

"I thought you said this was going to be difficult. So far it's been easy."

"It snowed everywhere but in the mountains. We have not been able to see much because of the trees. But if you noticed there have been a few landslides. I think most people think if it snows hard in the city it snows hard everywhere. This winter there was a lot of snow in Fairbanks, but as you can see none or very little in the mountains."

"Who is going to find out about that except you and me?"

"Exactly!" Jeb exclaimed. "So if anybody asks, milk it for all its worth."

The couple continued down the mountain. The closer they got to the bottom of the pass the deeper the snow became. They finally had to mount their horses and let them do the work of getting through the snow. After a while, they reached another frozen lake. Jeb stopped and dismounted. He drudged through the snow, grabbed Sharon's arm, and pulled her off her horse. Sharon literally fell off her horse onto the snow. Jeb pushed her down on her back and kissed her passionately. "We made it, Sharon, we made it."

When Sharon heard those words, she grabbed Jeb and kissed him passionately. "I knew we would," she yelled ecstatically.

Jeb helped Sharon to her feet. "The cabin is about a mile downstream from this lake."

CHAPTER 8

The couple arrived at the run-down cabin tired and hungry. Sharon helped carry in the supplies and after Jeb built a fire in the stove began fixing them something to eat. Jeb took the horses and the mule to the barn and took care of them. When he walked into the cabin, he sat down in a chair.

"I can't believe there was no snow on the mountain. It looked as if there thirty feet of snow."

Sharon walked over behind him and leaned over so she could put the side of her face on top of his head. "I am glad we made it. But I am still cold."

"Some warm water and food will warm you up. I may warm you up tonight," he said laughing as he pulled Sharon around the chair so she was sitting on his lap. "What's the matter?"

Sharon put her arms around his neck, lay her head on his shoulder, and kissed his neck. "I made my first husband wait. It would not be fair to let you have me before...."

A look of disappointment crossed Jeb's face. He smiled. "That's what I like about you. You put your cards on the table and we play by your rules. What are you going to do when I get tired of playing by your rules?"

Sharon laid her head back on his shoulder. "I hope you would do what is best for both of us. This is not a hurting game, this is life and respecting one another is part of life. Could you honestly do it knowing I would not want to, yet do it to please you? How much respect would there be for me? How much would you respect yourself?"

Jeb pushed Sharon off his lap and walked over to the window, "You're making it hard for me. You're a desirable woman and I love you. But how can I wait? There's only one bed for crying out loud."

Sharon walked back over to the stove. She continued cooking and never left the stove until the meat was cooked. She put a plate where she and Jeb would be sitting. She put food on the plates and sat down.

Jeb sat across from her and took her hand. "Provide me with a good life and I will wait. It's going to be hard, but I'll wait."

"I know it will be hard, as hard for you as it is for me. You have proven yourself to be a man and that's what I want in a husband. Yes, I will live with you in the cabin after we rebuild it. After we are married, you can have it whenever you want it. I not only want us to be lovers of one another s heart, but partners as well."

Jeb looked at Sharon with tender eyes. "You're worth waiting for," he whispered.

That night and several nights thereafter Jeb stayed up until Sharon was asleep. Occasionally, she would wake up long enough to lie on her side or she could lay her head on his shoulder. The nights always ended with 'I love you' from each of them.

When the supplies begin to get low, Jeb announced he was going into Wasatch to get more. Sharon prepared to go without asking him. She strolled into the barn dressed for the ride.

"Why is only one horse saddled?" she asked.

"I didn't know you were going. It's a twenty mile ride," Jeb said looking at Sharon

"Don't you want me to go?"

"You better, if something happens to me you'll be out here alone."

Jeb quickly saddled Sharon's horse and got the pack mule ready to go. They began the journey toward Wasatch. The creek wound its way down the mountainside on a gentle slope. It was toward evening when they arrived in the town. Jeb was glad to see the riverboat had made it as far as Wasatch.

"Go to the hotel and get you a room, tell the clerk you have been roaming around town and came in on the river boat. If they ask any questions, you're looking for Tom Skyler. I'll be along shortly, Jeb said as he dismounted. "Let me have your horse so I can take it to the stable." Sharon dismounted and started to hug him. "When we are in town we do not know one another."

"I forgot," Sharon said happily. "Is Tom Skyler as good looking as you are?"

"Naw, he's an old man," Jeb said grinning. "I think he is related to Methuselah."

Jeb went to the stables and had the horses taken care of. He walked slowly along the street so as not to attract attention to himself. He walked across the area where they were unloading the supplies from the boat. He started up the gangplank. When the Captain saw him, he waved a greeting. The two men met on the lower deck. Jeb followed the Captain to his cabin. When the door was closed, the two men hugged one another. "How's it going Jeb?"

"Not good, I am wanted for a murder I did not commit. I got a saloon girl attached to me. My cabins been burned. I am in a real mess."

"I can take you down river".

"I can't. The sheriff, the saloon owner and hard telling who else is killing off young men with mining accidents and putting their young wives to work in the saloon in Fairbanks and where else I do not know. I know two girls this has happened to."

"The one with you is one of them."

Jeb nodded. "There's another problem. I think I love her."

"Jeb! How do you do it?"

"How are Sally and the kids?"

"Their fine, Ted, the youngest boy gets into everything. Sarah is ten. You've never seen her. She was born a month or so after you left. Sally is doing well. She is as pretty as ever."

Jeb nodded. "I'm glad. Do you have a package for me?"

The Captain opened a drawer in his desk and handed Jeb a small package. "You know this is the last of it?"

"Have you had any trouble getting the money out of the bank?"

"None, whatsoever. Thanks for the new boat. It's a beauty."

"I'm glad you like it."

"The only thing is Sally doesn't like is when I come up to Alaska twice a year. But it's what makes our money."

"Tell sis I said, hello and give the kids a hug for me," Jeb said as he stood up.

"Joshua and Melissa are up here looking for me. I think they are nearly broke. If you see them, you never saw me."

The two men shook hands and Jeb left the boat and went to the hotel. He obtained a room and asked to see Tom Skyler.

"He is a popular man," the elderly woman clerk said smiling at Jeb. "There was a nice young lady that went up to see him a while ago."

Jeb nodded and went up to room 217. He stopped at the door when he heard laughing inside the room. He never knocked on the door but tried to open it and found it locked. He knocked on the door and the room became silent.

A few seconds later, Tom answered the door. Jeb stepped inside. The room was dingy with one chair and one bed. Sharon stood in front of the mirror adjusting her hair.

"You've got quite a girl there, you have," Tom said. "She told me she was running with you and she was a saloon girl. I figured you wouldn't mind sharing. This eye will be black in the morning I suppose."

"Let me look at it," Jeb said as he took hold of Tom s chin. "Is it your left eye?"

"Yep, it sure is," Tom said looking at Sharon.

Jeb bashed Tom in the right eye with his fist with such force it sent him falling to the floor.

"I'll share my tools, and my horses, but not my women, Jeb said as he pulled his friend to his feet. "What did she do to make you think I would share her with the likes of you?"

"Nothing," Tom said rubbing his eye. "Other than she said you sent her up here."

"Let me repeat, I'll share my tools and my horses, but not my women, especially with the likes of you."

Jeb quickly explained what had happened at the saloon and why Sharon was with him. Tom listened intently.

"Can we use your cabin till summer?"

"What if they decide to come looking for you over the pass?" Tom asked.

"With the stories you and I have told, they won't be coming over the pass, Jeb said as he walked over to Sharon. He turned her to face him. "You have been at this mirror primping since I walked in the door. If you're not going to at least say, 'hello' I'll leave.

"Oh," Sharon said softly. "Hello." Sharon sat on the bed. "You were talking business, a good wife dies not interfere when her husband is talking business."

Jeb scratched his beard. "That sounds good," he said. "I won't ask you for a kiss in front of ole Tom here. I don't want to embarrass him."

"Alright, I'll give you a kiss."

"No, not in front of Tom. It will embarrass him too much." Jeb turned to Tom. "Is there a good restaurant in town?"

"Yeah, there's one in the hotel, there's the saloon and one down on the end of the street.

"Which one's best?"

"I like the one at the end of the street. You past it when you came into town."

"Do you want to join us?"

"I ate a bit ago. But thanks!"

Jeb and Sharon left the hotel and walked slowly down the street. As they neared the saloon, Sharon grabbed Jeb's arm and hid her face on his chest.

"What's wrong?" Jeb asked knowing something had disturbed her greatly."

"That big man with the red beard in the brown shirt and black dirty pants is the man who suggested I talk to Mr. Elliot about a job."

"He's going into the saloon across the street. Let's eat and then we'll go to the saloon and pay him a visit," Jeb said as anger filled his voice.

CHAPTER 9

*T*HE COUPLE ATE A GOOD meal then walked to the saloon. They stopped at the door and looked inside. Mr. Elliot, the sheriff and the big man with the red beard were sitting at a table talking.

Jeb began putting two and two together. He took Sharon's hand and led her back to the hotel. They went back up to Tom Skyler s room. When Tom answered the door, Jeb pushed their way in.

"Elliot's men are in town," he said hurriedly. "If it does not snow the chances of your cabin being burned are very high. I'm sorry."

"Nothing to worry about," Tom said. "I ain't found enough gold in that creek to stay here this year. I'm moving anyway."

"I've got an idea."

"Not another one," Sharon moaned as she sat down on the bed.

"Sharon you stay here. Tom you remember, I share my horse, not my woman. I'll be back." Jeb said in anger.

Jeb gave Sharon a quick peck on the cheek and disappeared out the door.

Tom sat down on the bed next to Sharon. Sharon got up, walked over to the chair and sat in it.

"Ole Jeb been strange these last few years," Tom said. "He don't have much to do with people and then comes in town dragging you along. Can't figure out what got into him cause he used to hate women."

Sharon stood up. "I know Jeb told me to wait here for him. I am very uncomfortable being in this room alone with you. I think I will go down to the restaurant and get something to drink," she said as she glided across the room and stopped at the door.

"From what Jeb said, 'it would not be good for you to be alone.' I'll come with you." Tom said walking toward Sharon. Sharon gave him a hateful look. "I'll behave myself," Tom said softly. "And we'll talk about things you want to talk about. I'll look out for you while Jeb's gone."

Sharon agreed. The two of them went down to the restaurant and picked a table by the door so they could see Jeb when he returned. Sharon sat with her back to the door so she would not be recognized.

Jeb made his way back to the boat. He went to the Captain's cabin. He knocked on the door. The Captain opened the door. "Jeb, what a surprise!" He said smiling happily.

"Can you leave the ship?"

"Yes, why?" the Captain asked puzzled by Jeb's question.

"If a certain man gets on this ship to go up to Fairbanks, I want you to throw him overboard as a stowaway or Shanghai him."

"Why may I ask?"

"He is the man who kills the husbands of these young girls."

"You got it, let's go."

The Captain and Jeb stood outside the saloon as Jeb pointed the big man out.

The Captain's face turned to a scowl. "That man has also brought several young women up here on my boat. If it's possible he will be tossed half way between here and Fairbanks."

The two men shook hands and the Captain went back to his boat. Jeb looked around at the nearly deserted street then started for the hotel.

Jeb entered the hotel and passed the restaurant, not seeing Tom or Sharon.

"Jeb's back," he whispered. "You go ahead, I'll pay the bill."

"I'll wait for you," Sharon said. "My stomach tells me not to trust you."

Tom shrugged his shoulders and went over to pay the bill. They met Jeb in the hallway as he was coming back downstairs.

"Where have you been?"

"She didn't trust me, so we had some coffee."

Jeb smiled and turned around and started back up to the room.

Tom fell behind them. "Go on in the doors not locked."

Jeb sat down on the bed and Sharon sat beside him. "What did you find out?" Sharon asked as she took his hand.

"Tell it to Mr. Elliot," Tom said as entered the room and pulled out his revolver and aimed it at them.

"Tom," Jeb said in disbelief as he stood up. "Your part of it too?"

"No, Mr. Elliot said 'if he found out where you were to let him know or he would kill me.' I ain't taking any chances."

"Tom you're already a dead man," Jeb said trying to persuade his friend. "I'll bet he kills you not for bringing us to him, but will accuse you of something, in order to kill you."

"There you go talking like a lawyer." Tom said bitterly.

"He had an innocent man hung so he could frame Jeb and blame me for breaking jail. He is a ruthless killer!" Sharon exclaimed.

Sharon and I will go get on the boat. You can have her room. Change hotels do something besides making yourself a target. Just lay low for a few days," Jeb pleaded.

Tom agreed knowing he might be killed just for getting involved. Jeb and Sharon gathered their belongings. They told Tom they were getting on the boat to go back to Fairbanks, but went to another hotel instead.

The night clerk coughed when he saw them. "Yes," he said in a very sophisticated voice.

"We'd like a room. Mr. and Mrs. Nathan Perlinksy."

"That will be twenty-five dollars." The clerk said.

Jeb smiled. We do not want to be disturbed. "Here's a ten dollar tip that says we won't be."

"Very good sir," the clerk said giving Jeb the key to their room.

Jeb and Sharon went up to their room and locked the door. The room had beautiful furniture and curtains. The walls were painted blue with white trimming.

Jeb lay down on the bed. "Come here," he said extending his hand toward her.

Sharon sat down in the chair. "Jeb," she whispered. "I love you, but I am tired of putting up with the antics of a man who acts just like the men at the saloon. I am going to stay here and go back to California on the money you gave me."

Jeb sat up. "You can't mean that!"

Sharon nodded her head. "My husband treated me with respect before we were married. You do to an extent. Rather than fight you every night, I would rather be alone in California."

Jeb walked over to the saddlebags. "Here's your money," he said throwing it on the floor. Sharon knelt down to pick up the money. "I promised you a couple thousand. Take this with you, it will help," he added tossing her the biggest chunk of gold he had. When Jeb dropped the rock in front of her, she was amazed that Jeb would give it to her. She picked it up and looked at it and looked up at Jeb.

"It's pure gold," he said gathering up his things. "Take it you'll need it." Jeb opened the door and looked back down at Sharon.

Anger became etched on Sharon's face. She stood up, walked over to Jeb and slapped him. "You can't have your way with me so you're going to be like a spoiled brat and walk out on me. I'm glad; you have wasted enough of my time." She threw the gold and his money back on the floor. "I don't want your money. It's just a dirty as you are."

Jeb closed the door and walked over to her. He turned her around to face him. She pushed his arms away when he tried to put them around her. "I'm not going anywhere. A woman like you is too hard to find."

"Do you really mean that?"

"I love you Sharon and your throwing away how much money away I don't know, made me love you even more."

"I don't care about the gold," Sharon whispered as a tear streaked down her cheek. "All I want is for us to be someplace where we can be happy."

CHAPTER 10

*T*OM WALKED INTO THE SALOON. He stopped at the door and looked inside. He saw Mr. Elliot sitting at a table with two other men. He walked over to the table.

"Mr. Elliot," he said nervously. "Jeb and this lady are taking the boat back to Fairbanks."

"Thank you Tom," Mr. Elliot said reaching into his pocket. "Here's your money, plus a bonus."

"Thank you Mr. Elliot," Tom said smiling as he counted the money.

As Tom walked out of the saloon, Mr. Elliot nodded to the big man with the beard. He left the saloon and followed Tom down the street. When he was in a dark portion of the street, the man shot Tom in the back, killing him. The man ran up to him went through his pockets, took the money and disappeared in the darkness of the space between two buildings.

Jeb heard the shot and ran to the window. The street was dark and very little could be seen. He turned to Sharon. "I imagine they shot Tom, just because he knew something. I am discovering Mr. Elliot is a good double-crosser."

Sharon laid her head on Jeb's shoulder. "How can they be stopped?"

"I don't know," Jeb said quietly. "But they have to be."

"Let's go back to California," she pleaded.

"I love it up here," Jeb said as he looked out the window. "I especially like the valley where my cabin used to be. Before daylight, we will head back to Fairbanks. I have an idea."

"Oh, no, not another one," she moaned.

The next morning, the couple was on their way to Fairbanks. They were bundled in their winter clothes. The mule carried their supplies and extra blankets. That night they camped beside a small stream. Jeb spread a canvas so they would stay dry. Jeb true to his promise kissed her good night. That night they slept close together, for warmth.

Late the following evening they arrived in Fairbanks. They could see the boat at the dock. To Sharon's surprise, they went to the sheriff's house. Jeb pounded on the back door until the sheriff answered it. When he opened, the door Jeb shoved his revolver in the sheriff's face. "Back up," Jeb ordered as he forced his way into the house. "Lay down on the floor and give me your handcuffs." Jeb handcuffed the sheriff's hands behind his back and gagged him.

Sharon woke up the sheriff's wife and tied her hands behind her, gagged her and tied her feet together. Jeb took care of the horses and the mule. When he came back into the house, he found the sheriff's wife laying on the floor with a blanket thrown over her. Sharon was in the bed asleep. Jeb smiled because he knew she had, had a few hard days. He went into the front room and dragged the sheriff into the bedroom. He threw a blanket over him.

"We'll have a chat in the morning," Jeb said as he knelt beside the sheriff. "Right now I am going to get some sleep."

Jeb kissed Sharon on the cheek. He looked at her in the soft light of the lamp and kissed her again. "I am one lucky fellow," he thought to himself. He lay down beside her. A few minutes later, he felt Sharon snuggle up to him

"I love you," she whispered.

The next morning Sharon woke Jeb up with a kiss on the cheek. As he sat up, she handed him a cup of coffee. "Thank you," he whispered. "Since you're up, is everybody still tied up?"

"Yes, and I have done nothing to help them." She said.

"I doubt the sheriff's wife is on the caper. But we know the sheriff is and he had better start talking." He turned to Sharon. "How well can you impersonate an old woman?"

"I don't know," she said with hesitation. "Have you got another idea?" she asked shaking her head in disbelief.

"You could be on the lookout just by walking to the store."

"After the saloon opens I'm going to be an old man. I know you want to rescue Sandy." Jeb said softly.

"Not at the risk of your life." Sharon argued.

"Everything is going to be okay," Jeb whispered.

Jeb began putting powder on his hair and beard. He went through his clothes and put on the shabbiest one's he had. "How do I look?"

"Old and you stink," Sharon said making a face at Jeb.

"Good! Get me a bottle of whiskey out of the sheriff's supply. I imagine he has to drink a lot to clear his conscience." Jeb tucked the bottle in his belt. "I'll be back."

Sharon grabbed Jeb and kissed him passionately. "Please be careful."

Jeb went out the back door and stayed behind the buildings until he was next to the saloon. He took the bottle of whiskey and poured most of it out. He took a drink, sloshed it around in his mouth and spit it out. He walked into the saloon. The girls were sitting at the tables waiting for customers. Mr. Elliot was nowhere to be seen. Jeb saw Sandy sitting at a table by herself with a full bottle of whiskey in front of her. He staggered over to it and sat down.

"How's my favorite wee little lass this morn-en?" he slurred. "Stand up and turn around." Sandy did as she was told. "Oh my," Jeb said happily. "Yer purty and yer little and that's the way I like-em. How much are ya?"

"Ten dollars." Sandy said nervously.

"That's ah bit expensive, but I'll bet you're worth every dime," Jeb slurred. "I like mine in the morn-en after ah gals had a chance to rest. Shall we?"

Sandy knew better than to say 'no,' she had said, 'no' to one drunk and was lock in a room in the dark with no food or water for two days. Sandy nodded as she stood up from the table.

Jeb took hold of Sandy's hand as he had trouble standing up. "I had a wee bit much to drink. Yer gonna haf to guide me."

Sandy led Jeb up to her room. When Jeb closed the door Sandy started to take off her dress. "Leave it on," Jeb whispered. Sandy looked at him strangely when his accent disappeared. Jeb pulled Sandy close to him and covered her mouth with his hand. "I can't let you scream. I am a friend of Sharon's. She is sorta safe. She wants to know if you want out of here bad enough to let me help you. I know they killed your husband and Sharon's husband and double-crossed you to make you work here. Do you want out?"

Sandy looked at Jeb with disbelief in her eyes and nodded her head. 'Yes,' "Humph," Sandy said her voice muffled by Jeb's hand. Jeb took his hand a short distance from her mouth, as he did not trust her...

"How," she asked anxiously.

"We haven't got that figured out yet," Jeb said as he stepped back from her. "But if you want out, we will get you out."

"I want to go back home. But I can't save any money. What do I have to do?" Sandy asked.

"Quit drinking," Jeb ordered. "You need to be sober for this event."

Sandy nodded. "But Mr. Elliot likes for me to drink in the morning while he talks to me. He brags about how good I was."

"Like Sharon does," he whispered. "Be ready to go tonight. It may not be tonight, but be ready. Pack the clothes you want to take."

"All I have are saloon dresses."

Jeb nodded as he sat on the bed. "We have to be here for at least a half an hour. Kneel down in front of me." Sandy knelt in front of him. He began messing up her hair and smearing her make up. "The living conditions may not be the best, but you will be out of here." He took out his knife and cut one of the straps to her dress. He cupped her face in his hands and looked at her coldly. "Not a word of this to anyone. I am risking my life for you. No drinking."

"I understand," she said as she laid her head in his lap. "I thank you."

"Take off your clothes and throw them in a pile and get in bed. All you have to do is pretend how good it was." Jeb left Sandy after he was in her room for half an hour. He swaggered down the stairway. "She's a wild little lass, she was." He stopped at the table where the other girls were sitting. "The little ones are the best. That little gals in heaven on account of me." Jeb swaggered out the door. The girls ran up to Sandy's room fearing the worst.

Jeb made his way back to the sheriff's house. "Has anyone been looking for him?"

"Not yet," Sharon said quietly. "What about Sandy?"

"She wants out, but I think Mr. Elliot has her addicted to alcohol so bad, she may tell him we are going to try and get her out. It will be a day or two before we try it. I want to make sure Elliot does not post any guards to wait for me."

CHAPTER 11

That night Jeb was watching the back of the saloon to see if any guards were posted to capture him. He had Sharon waiting with the horses in the dark shadows of another building.

Jeb was surprised to see Mr. Elliot lead Sandy out of the saloon. She was blindfolded, gagged and her hands were tied behind her back. The men left Mr. Elliot and Sandy alone. Jeb knew this would not be a good time to try to rescue Sandy because too many people were to close. He decided to see where Sandy was going to be taken.

Mr. Elliot led Sandy back behind the buildings to the edge of town and a very large house. He led her up to the back door and knocked on it. A few minutes later, a short fat man answered the door. The three went inside the house. Jeb crept along the edge of the house until he was at a window of the room where Sandy was taken. Jeb became angry when Mr. Elliot shoved Sandy into a plush cushioned chair.

The fat man stood in front of her and took the gag out of her mouth. Jeb checked to see if there were any guards then put his ear close to the window.

"The boss wants to know who you was with this morning!"

"I don't know," she cried. The fat man slapped her. "I don't know, he had a strange accent." The fat man slapped her again.

"This is going to go on until you tell us or your dead," Mr. Elliot hissed. "Who was he?"

The fat man picked up a bottle of whiskey. He handed it to Mr. Elliot and walked behind Sandy. The fat man grabbed Sandy by the hair and pulled her head back over the top of the chair. Mr. Elliot poured some whiskey into Sandy's mouth and then forced it shut forcing Sandy to swallow. Mr. Elliot forced the whiskey down her three times. After each drink, the fat man slapped her from behind. The whiskey began to take effect.

"Who were you with this morning?"

"I don't know," Sandy said crying. "Please don't hit me again," She pleaded as the tears streaked her make up.

"Who was he?" Mr. Elliot yelled in her ear.

"I don't know," Sandy cried. "He never told me his name."

The fat man slapped her again.

"Who was he?"

"I don't know," Sandy cried as the tears flowed freely. "He was a friend of Sharon's."

The fat man and Mr. Elliot looked at one another in disbelief. Mr. Elliot stuffed the gag back in Sandy's mouth. The two men went into another room where Jeb could see them, but could not hear them. Mr. Elliot came out the room grabbed Sandy by the hair, dragged her out of the house and down the alley by her hair. Just as Jeb was ready to jump Mr. Elliot, he heard two men running to meet him. Mr. Elliot shoved Sandy into the waiting arms of a tall slender man.

"The boss wants you to take her up in the mountains and let her be cold for a day or two, then kill her," Mr. Elliot said laughing. "The boss has had his fun with her so have all the fun you want. Just make sure her body can't be found."

The two men tried to get Sandy on her horse. She kicked at them as best she could. Tom grabbed her leg and pulled it upward. He began laughing. Jeb was itching to help Sandy but there were too many people that would hear the gunshots.

Mr. Elliot came out of the saloon. "Can't you do anything right?" He said loudly his voice filled with anger. He grasped Sandy by the throat and began choking her. "Are you going to get on this horse?" Sandy nodded her head 'yes.' Mr. Elliot let go of her throat. Sandy allowed the two men to help her into the saddle. "I hated to do this to you Sandy, but the boss figures you're too big of a risk. Have fun fella's. If she escapes, its prison, so she has to die."

Mr. Elliot went into the saloon. Jeb was making his way to where Sharon was waiting when two more men left the saloon.

"Sandy's been slapped around a bit," he whispered. "They are taking her up into the mountains. We will follow them and rescue Sandy in a while."

Sandy sat on the horse as it made its way along the trail. She could not see or beg for her life. She began to wonder if it had all been a trap so the fat man could get rid of her. She hoped that somewhere, somehow, someone would help her.

"You know she is cute," Jack said as he took the reins of Sandy's horse and slapped her leg with them.

"I brought along enough supplies for three days, so we know we will be gone that long. Poor little thing will be glad to get close to us when she gets cold. Ain't that right, you little witch," Tom said backhanding Sandy across the face.

Sandy sat crying after Tom hit her. She wondered why that man ever came to see her. If he was going to rescue her, why was it taking him so long?

"How we gonna figure who gets her first," Tom said.

"That is easy, I'm the oldest," Jake said. "Did you bring some whiskey?"

"Enough to keep her drunk for three days."

The trail passed between two large rock outcroppings on either side of the road.

"Aaaaagh!" Jack screamed as he clutched his chest and fell from his horse.

Tom dismounted and ran to his brother. As he was kneeling beside him, Jeb came around the rock and smashed him with the rifle in the head. Tom fell beside his brother, dead.

Jeb took the knife out of Jacks chest, ran to Sandy's horse and grabbed the reins. "How is my favorite wee little lass this morn-en?" Sandy's heart leaped for joy. Jeb cut Sandy's hands free.

Sharon ran out of the bushes and grabbed the reins to Sandy's horse. "It's Sharon," she said loudly, "your safe now." She led the horse back into the bushes, helped Sandy dismount, took off her blindfold, and took the gag out of her mouth.

"Scream loud," Jeb whispered loudly. "The louder the better."

Sandy screamed as loud and as long as she could. The two riders following the three at a distance heard Sandy screaming. They began laughing and slowed their horses to a walk. As they approached the rocks, they saw two horses with empty saddles. They saw the two men lying on the ground and dismounted.

One man got off his horse and ran over to them and knelt beside them. "Their dead," he said as he began looking around the rocks.

Sandy screamed. The two men drew their guns and Jeb open fire with his rifle. He walked slowly down the hill to where the four men lay dead.

Sandy and Sharon joined him. "I'm sorry I let you go through so much," Jeb said apologetically. "Now, I know who the boss is and I am really sorry about you getting beaten so badly. There just was not the opportunity to rescue you till now."

"I'm free of him that's all I care about," Sandy said crying as she clung to Sharon.

"If you ladies will help me get these men on their horses, I will take them to town and give them to Mr. Elliot."

When the men were draped across their saddles Jeb took the girls to an abandoned mine and told them he would be back. Jeb rode the trail in a hurry. When he arrived in Fairbanks, Jeb tied the reins of the dead men s horses to the hitching rail. He fired several shots into the air and rode out of town as fast as his horse would carry him. He joined Sharon and Sandy and each of them greeted him with a hug.

"Can either one of you shoot a rifle?"

"I can," Sandy said softly. "But with my eye swollen shut I don't see how I could hit anything."

Jeb put his arm around Sandy and gave her a hug. "If I had known what I know now, we would have tried a different way." Jeb walked over to Sharon. "There's no need to get jealous," he whispered. "After what she's been through, she needed some encouragement. Can you shoot a rifle?"

"No, but I can learn," Sharon said hoping he would teach her.

"We haven't got enough ammunition for me to teach you, but I can show you how to sight your target." Jeb patiently showed Sharon the ins and outs of handling a rifle. "If we get in a gunfight it's important to keep them pinned down. I'll pick them off as I can."

CHAPTER 12

The bartender heard a noise outside the saloon. When he saw the four dead bodies, he ran to Mr. Elliot's room and beat on the door. Mr. Elliot opened the door in his nightclothes. "What's the matter with you?"

"You're not going to believe what's out in front of the saloon."

Mr. Elliot dressed quickly and hurried to the front of the saloon. As he stepped out the door and saw four horses with the four bodies of his men, his mouth fell open and the cigar fell from his mouth. He bowed his head and rubbed his face with his hands. "This man is good," he said as he walked back in the saloon and sat at a table and began drinking.

It was close to noon when Joshua came riding into town. He dismounted and hurried into the saloon. He sat down uninvited at Mr. Elliot's table. "Mr. Elliot, can we make a deal?"

"It depends on what it is."

"This is what I want. I want Jeb's body to take back to San Francisco. This way several large projects can be started with the money Jeb has left behind."

"So you know where they are at?"

"I can take you there," Joshua said enthusiastically.

Mr. Elliot flipped the ashes off his cigar. "You would take me there just to have Jeb's body. Joshua nodded. "Tell me," Mr. Elliot said with a mischievous grin. "Isn't your wife the one who has dark short hair and is abundant," he asked circling his hands over his chest.

"Yes, why?" Joshua asked puzzled that Mr. Elliot would be interested in his wife.

"I want to congratulate you on having the fine sense to pick a fine woman like that. Oh, that I could be so lucky," he added looking up at the ceiling and then at Joshua's smiling face. "Sure you can have Jeb's body. I won't need it. When can we leave?"

"As soon as you're ready," Joshua said happily. "I'll go tell Melissa goodbye."

"You do that my boy, you do that," he said nodding at the big man with the red beard. "We'll be waiting." The big man with the beard nodded back. It was not long until Mr. Elliot and the gang were headed for the abandoned mine.

Sharon walked back into the mine as far as the light would let her go. She lit a candle.

"What's in this box?"

Jeb opened it. "Dynamite, but it's hard telling how old it is and if it will explode. Let's make a few dummies." Jeb began emptying out some of the sticks of dynamite and put good-sized rocks in hem and attaching a fuse to them.

"How do you know they will be coming?" Sandy asked.

"I have killed four of his men; you two are the only witnesses to what he has done."

"Would you sit back and drink whiskey or kill those who could put you out of business?"

"I would hunt you down." Sandy said sadly. "I was always blinded folded when I was taken to the fat man's house. He took out my gag so he could kiss me and hit me, if I did not return his kisses. I learned to survive. I do not know who he is, but I want to kill him."

"I can't let you do that."

"But I will," she whispered. "The way you and Sharon look at one another a person would think you love one another."

"I love him," Sharon said coldly. "But with him, I think its pure lust."

"That's not true," Jeb said, defending himself. "I love you; it's just hard for me to say it. Besides a man would have to love you to put up with what I have had to put up with for the last week or so."

"You have that just exactly backwards," Sharon said as she hugged Jeb. She started to kiss him, but he pushed her away.

"Here they come!" he said trying to count them. "Looks like about seven, make every shot count as best you can."

"Jeb Pearson," Joshua yelled. "We are here to kill you, so I can take your body back to San Francisco. Mr. Elliot promised, if you let the girls go and they will be treated fairly."

"Upon hearing, those words Sandy braced her rifle on a rock and aimed her rifle at Mr. Elliot. She pulled the trigger and Mr. Elliot was knocked from his saddle to the ground by the force of the bullet in his stomach.

"Kill them," Mr. Elliot yelled as pain racked his body.

The men began moving up the rocks toward the mine entrance. Jeb ran back in the mine and released the brake on an old oar car. While he was shooting at the advancing gang, Sharon and Sandy began pushing the oar car toward the entrance of the mine. When it ran out of track, it toppled down the steep hillside toward the gang. While the men were running to get out of the way of the bouncing car, Jeb was shooting them down.

Joshua was making his way along the cliff to get above Jeb and the girls. Mr. Elliot saw him and signaled the man with the red beard. As he was aiming at Joshua, Sharon was aiming at him. The man fired and Joshua fell to the ground. Sharon fired and the bullet hit the rock next to the man imbedding chips of rocks in his face. He screamed as he covered his face and blood ran between his fingers. Sandy took aim and fired sending him backwards with a bullet in his chest. He staggered and fell face fist into the creek.

Mr. Elliot was hiding and could not be seen. Sandy was specifically looking for him, but shooting at other men as well.

Jeb threw a stick of dynamite and it landed near what remained of the gang. They ran and hid among the rocks. When it did not explode one of the men went to investigate and was promptly shot.

"Get them," Mr. Elliot yelled shooting at his own men.

The men started back up the rocky slope toward the mine. Jeb lit the fuse to another stick of dynamite. He waited until the fuse was short and then threw it. The men began running back down the slope. The dynamite exploded just above their heads and sent the three of them falling to the ground. The only return fire was coming from Mr. Elliot.

"Get ready girls," Jeb said as he lit the fuse. "This one is wet and may not do anything but create smoke. Keep Elliot pinned down." The girls began rapid fire at Mr. Elliot's hiding place. When the dynamite landed near him, he got up and started running. Sandy and Sharon began shooting at him. He stumbled and fell. The dynamite exploded. He screamed and fell among the rocks. "Stay down girls this may not be over yet," Jeb said as he walked to the entrance of the mine. He scanned the area looking for any movement. There was none. He climbed over to Joshua and stood over his body. He looked down at it. "Whatever deal he made with you, it was to get Melissa in the saloon."

Sharon hurried down to where the man with the red beard lay face down. She walked up behind him and when she was several feet from him, she aimed and shot him three more times. Sharon sat down on a rock and started crying.

Jeb climbed the rocks over to Sharon. He put his arm around her. "I know he killed your husband and I don't blame you for what you did."

Another rifle shot broke the silence. Jeb looked over at Sandy. "It's Mr. Elliot. He was alive," she yelled.

Jeb gathered the two girls around him. "I have an idea."

"Here we go again," Sharon said as she took a deep sigh. "You and your ideas."

"I'm gonna carry these men up close to the mine shaft and then we'll blow it. You know a mining accident." The girls smiled happily.

CHAPTER 13

That afternoon the trio rode into town. They stopped at the sheriff's house. The house was empty of any occupants. It appeared that someone left in a hurry.

"Did either one of you see the sheriff at the mine?" Jeb asked as he went through some papers. He found a sheriff's badge and pinned it on.

"I did." Sharon said looking the disarray of the house. "I shot at him, but never saw him after that."

"Sandy make sure that rifle is loaded," Jeb said coldly. "We are going after the fat man."

"Who is it?" Sandy asked her voice filled with curiosity and hate.

"The mayor."

"The mayor!" both girls said in disbelief.

The trio walked down the street each carrying a rifle. The town s people knew there was trouble, but had no idea what kind. They had never seen such a sight. Sharon was wearing her long beige dress and a heavy winter coat. Sandy her yellow low cut saloon dress and a long coat. Jeb was wearing a sheriff's badge on his winter coat. As they approached the mayor's house, he looked out the window and saw them coming. He ran out to his barn and began hitching up his buggy. The trio went into the front room and made their way through the house. They exited the house out the back door. Jeb heard a nose in the barn and motioned the girls to go on either side of the door. Jeb opened the door.

"What's the idea of barging in on me like this?" the mayor said nervously. "My, young lady what happened to your face?" he asked when he saw Sandy.

"You know what happened to my face, you creep," Sandy yelled leveling her rifle at him.

"I can assure you it was not me, I am a law abiding citizen."

"Naw," Jeb said. "I watched you slap her while she was blindfolded with her hands tied behind her back. Then you had Mr. Elliot pour whiskey down her in order to make her talk. You liked her looks so you had the man with the red beard kill her husband. Mr. Elliot lied to her about a job and she was brought to your house in the middle of the night on numerous occasions. What have I left out?"

The mayor was wiping the perspiration off his face. He reached inside his coat pocket and Sandy pulled the trigger. The mayor was knocked backwards by the bullet with a stomach wound. As he lay on the ground, Sandy emptied the rifle of its shells and began beating him with the butt of her rifle. "I hate you," she screamed repeatedly. Jeb did nothing to stop her. Finally, Sandy fell to the ground exhausted. The mayor was dead. Jeb helped her to her feet as she sobbed and cried. Jeb took Sandy to the hotel. He asked the lady to give Sandy a bath and take care of her. Sharon went to the saloon and found Sandy a better dress to wear in public.

While Sandy was being cleaned up, Sharon and Jeb went to the boat dock. They searched among the passengers waiting to get on the boat. He saw the sheriff sitting on a trunk. Jeb walked over to him.

"Come on Sheriff, you're going back to face the consequences."

"All I did was look the other way," the sheriff said sadly.

"Yes, you looked the other way while men were being murdered and young women were turned into prostitutes," Jeb said coldly.

"Look," the sheriff said quietly. "I am an old man; I needed the money to take care of my wife."

"You're coming back with me," Jeb said as he grabbed the sheriff's arm.

"Let him go," the sheriff's wife said as she aimed a revolver at Jeb. "We are getting on that boat and going to California."

"Since you got the gun, I guess you're right," Jeb said rubbing the back of his neck.

Jeb saw Sharon walking up behind the sheriff's wife. "Drop it or die," Sharon whispered jamming the rifle into the sheriff's wife back. "I am not going to let you interfere with my marriage to Jeb," Sharon said taking the revolver from the sheriff's hand.

"What part did you play in all this?"

"I was told someone wanted that short girl and I was to keep her in the dark and feed her. So I did."

"You were well paid?"

"You did look the other way didn't you? And wearing a sheriff's badge," Jeb said disgusted by the whole thing. "I am actually a lawyer and it will be a pleasure to prosecute your case."

"You have no witnesses." The sheriff said.

"The girls." Jeb replied.

"Who is going to believe a whore?" The sheriff asked laughing.

"We'll find out won't we?" Jeb said as he took the sheriff by the arm and led him and his wife to the jail.

When they were in a jail cell, Jeb looked at them long and hard. The only reason I put you in the same cell is because you're married. If the people of this town believe Sharon, Sandy and a few other girls you will hang. If you want to save the town a trial, this revolver has two bullets. I'll tell folks you left on the boat after resigning. That way your name can stay in good standing. The girls and I will bury you, but there will be no funeral. Let me know what you decide."

Jeb went to the bank. He ordered everyone out of the bank until the following morning. The people complained, but left one by one when he drew his revolver. He ordered the tellers to leave also. He walked into the president's office. The banker and his secretary were working.

"Sharon take this lady, tie her up and gag her as well. I don't want her screaming." Sharon took the protesting lady out of the office at the point of a gun.

"What do you want?" a tall, heavy set, balding man demanded as he stood up.

"Mr. Elliot is dead," Jeb said as he sat in a chair. He tried to kill two ladies and me; unfortunately he was buried, in a landslide at a cliff that was not very stable."

"How can I believe that?"

"I'll let you dig him and five other men out from under the rocks." Jeb took out his revolver and aimed it at the banker. I want all Mr. Elliot's money and the saloon transferred to my name dated ten days ago. I believe you knew what was going on with obtaining young women for the saloon because you handled the paper work. I will give you twenty thousand dollars to get you to California free. You'll be a free man instead of a dead one.

The banker sat down in his chair and began shuffling papers. Jeb signed the transfer papers and the deed to the saloon.

"We'll go to your house and get your clothes and I'll take you to the Captain who is a friend of mine." When they arrived at the banker's house, he began stuffing clothes into two carrying cases. When they were ready to leave Jeb noticed the banker had not opened one closet. When he opened it, he found it full of women's clothes. "Whose are these?"

"My secretary stayed with me once in a while." Mr. Langsford answered.

"Does she have a name?"

"Mrs. Elliot!" The banker answered.

"The saloon owner's wife?" Jeb ask confounded by his answer.

"Yes," the banker answered. "He ignored her after he got the saloon."

"She's not that bad of a looking woman." Jeb said.

"True, but the saloon had younger and prettier ones."

Jeb nodded.

The banker and Jeb left the house and walked to the boat dock. They walked up the gangplank and were greeted by the Captain.

"Captain," Jeb said coldly. "This is Mr. Langsford, the banker. Mr. Langsford, this is the Captain of this ship. Can we go to your cabin?"

"Certainly," the Captain said wondering why Jeb had brought this man aboard. When they arrived at the cabin, the three men sat down.

"I brought this man to you Captain for his protection," Jeb said happily. "He is carrying twenty thousand dollars and I am wondering if you would keep it in the safe for him. That way he can enjoy the voyage and not have to worry about someone stealing his money."

The Captain smiled. "Certainly. I can do that for him."

Mr. Langsford gave the Captain the money and watched as he put it in the safe. "There you are my good man, it is safe. You may get it any time you want. See a Mr. Trebble and he will give you a cabin. He is the man on the lower deck assigning rooms. Just tell him the Captain said to give you a good room on the upper deck."

"What do you want me to tell Mrs. Elliot?" Jeb asked with a sneer on his face.

"I will send for her as soon as I get to California." He answered.

Mr. Langsford left the cabin. Jeb remained seated. "What is it Jeb?"

"Mr. Langsford knew about the situation at the saloon. I cannot pin anything on him because all he did was take care of the money and transfer the deeds of the mines. He also signed a dead man's assets including the saloon over to me, and I forged Mr. Elliot's name. I think he is in love with Mrs. Elliot or at least she was his mistress. Do you think if he got to drinking and was reminded of Mrs. Elliot he could jump overboard and try to swim to shore?"

"In these cold water's he would not last….more….than…a hundred feet," the Captain, said looking at the safe.

"Well Captain, I have to be going. So far as I know there is only one other person I have to deal with that knew about the saloon," Jeb said standing up and shaking the captain's hand.

"Oh, Jeb, the reason the man with the beard was not tossed overboard is because the three of them were always together."

"That's ok, he is dead."

Jeb walked back to the bank. He unlocked the door and found Sharon sitting in the president's chair and Mrs. Elliot tied up sitting on the floor behind the president's desk.

Jeb sat down on the floor in front of her. He took the gag out of her mouth. "What did you know about what was going on in the saloon?"

"Nothing!" she spat hatefully. "Mr. Langsford told me one day we would be rich, that's all he told me."

"What did your husband tell you?" Jeb asked.

"Nothing, we have not spoken for seven years. After he got the saloon and younger, prettier girls began working there, he quit coming home." Mrs. Elliot said sadly.

"Do you think you could run this bank and keep tabs on who makes what in the dividing of the money?" Jeb ask.

"Yes, I could do that easily." She answered.

"Good, you will work at the bank from 9:00am until 5:00pm. Then you will wait tables at the saloon for the men playing poker from 7:00pm to midnight. Your pay will be a room, your food, drinks and new clothes when you need them. You can play with the miners if you wish. Oh and Mr. Langsford said, "You're getting to old."

Mrs. Elliot nodded. "I guess so, since he is on his way to California and I am here."

CHAPTER 14

The next morning Jeb knocked on the door to Melissa's hotel room. She was startled to see Jeb standing at the door. He pushed the door open and walked into the room. He looked at the plush furnishings for an Alaska hotel.

"Got bad news about Joshua!" Jeb said toying with his hat.

"What could it be?" She asked.

"Joshua was always good at making deals. The trouble was he made them with the wrong people. He made a deal with you and it turned sour after you blackmailed him into marrying you. Considering the size of them that's probably the only good thing about you."

"Shut about me. What about Joshua?" She asked her voice full of hate.

"Joshua made a deal with the devil and one of the devil's men shot and killed him. The deal was, after I was killed, Joshua would get my body to take back to San Francisco where you would find out that I am broke. I don't have a dime."

"Get out of here!" Melissa ordered with hate in her voice.

"There's more." Mr. Elliot was part of a ring that killed off young woman's husbands and under dire circumstances put them to work in a saloon. When he saw your size he decided to make you a saloon girl and Joshua played right into his hands except that Mr. Elliot and all the gang dead. I bought the saloon."

"I thought you were broke!" Melissa yelled.

"In California I am broke. In Alaska I am well off."

Melissa looked at Jeb strangely. "So what if you own the saloon."

Jeb grinned from ear to ear. "I know how bad you want to get back to California. I also know you're broke. I also know you like to drink. I also know you liked to fool around on your husband and me. Here's what I will do. I will give you a place to live, all the food you want to eat, all the liquor you want and there will be plenty of men for you to play with."

"How much are you going to pay me?"

"I'm giving you everything you want in life, that's your pay. There will be a slight fee of seventy five percent of your evening with the boys. After that deal in California you owe me."

"You're rotten," Melissa screamed. "I'll find a job."

"Who is going to give you a job after they find out you wanted to work for me in the first place."

"You wouldn't!" She screamed.

"Yes, I would," Jeb, said laughing. "You double-crossed me, but in return I am giving you a job.

"But I'll never get back to California." She sobbed.

"Precisely, and I will never have to worry about someone coming to find me on a phony breaking out of jail charge. Shall we move your belongs to the saloon?"

Melissa looked at Jeb with pure hatred. "If I get the chance I will kill you."

"Oh, Melissa don't take it so hard," Jeb said laughing. "After a while you'll be having so much fun you'll forget all about California."

CHAPTER 15

Mr. Langsford and the Captain were celebrating Mr. Langsford getting out of Alaska. The more he drank the more he talked about the girls in the saloon. As the Captain found out his involvement with the way, the girls were double-crossed, the more the Captain disliked him. The Captain reminded him of Mrs. Elliot and he laughed saying she was getting to old. He reminded the Captain with the money he had he could find a younger woman. On his way, back to his cabin Mr. Langsford tripped and busted his head on a sharp metal post on one of the stairways. Since there were no facilities for a funeral aboard the ship, his body was tossed overboard.

The sheriff shot his wife in the head and then committed suicide. Jeb, Sharon and Sandy took their bodies to an abandoned mine and laid them at the base of the cliff. Jeb went to the top and buried several sticks of dynamite. He lit the fuse and ran. The explosion ripped into the side of the mountain. Rocks and trees tumbled down its slopes burying the sheriff and his wife's bodies. As the dust cleared, Jeb walked over to his horse.

Sandy stood at the edge of the cliff watching the landslide. She turned to Sharon. "What makes good men go bad?"

"In the sheriff's case it was money, in the mayor's case it was something he wanted but could not have, but got it any way he could," Sharon said sadly.

Jeb mounted his horse and started down the mountain. "You two coming?"

"We'll be along," Sharon said walking over to Jeb. Sandy wants to talk.

Jeb started down the mountain and saw someone through the trees. He hid in the bushes and waited. When the rider came into view, he drew his revolver. "Freeze," he yelled when the rider was passed him. "Who are you?"

"Mrs. Elliot," she said in a terrified voice.

Jeb spurred his horse forward until he was beside her. "What are you doing way up here?"

"Following you," she said softly.

"Why?" Jeb asked as he put his revolver back in its holster.

"Jeb, since Mr. Langsford left I have no one to talk to and I was wondering if….."

"The girls are over there, ask them." Jeb turned his horse to go down the mountain. He stopped and watched Mrs. Elliot dismount and walk over to where Sharon and Sandy were standing.

"What do you want?" Sandy asked bitterly as she glared hatefully at Mrs. Elliot.

"I'm sorry about what happened to you," Mrs. Elliot said sadly, as she reached for Sandy's hand. Sandy pulled her hand away from Mrs. Elliot and backed away from her. "I didn't know what he was doing. After there were younger and prettier girls he never came home." She turned to face Sharon. "I hope the same thing does not happen to you."

"I made him a promise," Sharon said happily. "It had better keep him home!" she exclaimed as she looked in Jeb's direction with narrowed eyes.

Mrs. Elliot smiled a weak smile. "I am lonesome and need a friend. Two would be better."

Sharon put her arm around Mrs. Elliot and gave her a hug. "Sandy and I have been there we know how you feel."

"You really didn't know?" Sandy asked.

"No," she answered sadly. "I hadn't spoken to my husband in seven years. I was with Mr. Langsford."

Sandy stepped over to Mrs. Elliot and gave her a hug. "We can be friends," she said with some reservation.

Jeb had hidden behind a large bush where he could watch the ladies. He smiled happily when he saw Sandy give Mrs. Elliot a hug. "Let's go ladies; we got a saloon to open."

"Quit being in a hurry Jeb, we girls have a wedding to plan. Remember?"

"You know we don't get any business until in the afternoon," Sandy said emphatically.

"Alright," Jeb said as he smiled, knowing he was beaten. "But the bank opens at ten and the saloon at noon. They had best open on time." Jeb continued down the mountain followed by three chattering women as they planned Jeb and Sharon's wedding.

Two weeks later in the little white church at the edge of town, Sharon and Jeb were married. It was a highly private ceremony with Sharon, Jeb, Sandy, Mrs. Elliot in attendance. The ceremony was brief and within a few minutes Jeb had a wife and he intended for her to keep her promise.

As they were leaving the church, Melissa strolled casually up to Jeb. "I have something for you," she said giving him a coy little smile.

Jeb knew not to trust Melissa. "What is it?" Jeb asked watching the movement of Melissa's hands.

"This," she said swinging a full bottle of whiskey at Jeb. Jeb ducked.

The bottle barely missed hitting Sharon in the face. "You little hussy," Sharon screamed as she grabbed Melissa by the hair and began jerking her from one side to the other. She straightened Melissa up and hit her in the face with her fist. Melissa fell backwards, stumbled on a tree root and fell to the ground. "You may work at the saloon, but you leave me and Jeb alone."

Melissa stood up. "You promised you would marry me," she screamed hysterically at Jeb. "You run all over Alaska with her and decide she is better than me."

"She is better than you in more ways than one," Jeb said taking Sharon's hand. "Now get back to the saloon and earn your pay before I decide to take more of your money for damages to my marriage."

"When I get back to California, you're going to pay dearly for this!"

Sharon looked at Jeb with fear in her eyes. "What can she do Jeb?"

"I can do plenty," Melissa screamed as she got up from the ground. "If I have to I'll prostitute myself all the way to San Francisco to see you back in jail."

"Get back to work!" Jeb ordered.

"I'm going," Melissa said hatefully. "It may take me a year, but I will get back to California."

Jeb smiled weakly at Sharon. "I have an idea," he whispered.

"Oh, no," Sharon said helplessly. "Not another one."

Jeb smiled a wicked smile. "This one will get rid of Melissa," he whispered.

Sharon smiled a huge smile and her face beamed with happiness. "Can I help?"

"It depends on if she falls for it or not."

"You're not going to kill her are you?" Sharon asked hesitating with each word.

Jeb shook his head. 'No,' he said smiling. "If you think she hates me now, wait a while."

CHAPTER 16

The summer was cooler than most of the miners could remember for many years.

The first snowfall occurred the last of September and by the middle of October, the town was buried with snow. It was also crowded with miners who had left their mines early. They cashed in their gold and silver and spent their money freely on the girls and liquor.

Jeb and Sharon were also disappointed because they had to leave the house they were building almost finished. It was sitting on a small knoll overlooking the creek and the facing the spot where the old cabin had stood. It was with great reluctance they left the inside of the cabin unfinished.

The saloon was filled to capacity every night. The more it snowed the more men flocked to the saloon in search of food. Jeb had thought he ordered enough food to last the winter but by November, he was wondering if he had or not.

Sharon worked in the kitchen as a cook. Sandy growing tired of Melissa stealing her tips and asked if she could work in the kitchen as well. Melissa worked from noon until midnight. Mrs. Elliot came in from the bank at seven in the evening to wait on tables. Mrs. Elliot kept the tables where the men were playing poker supplied with food. Melissa kept the other part of the saloon supplied with drinks, as did several other girls.

Mrs. Elliot did not try to keep up with Melissa and her flirting ways. Since her fling and being dumped by Mr. Langsford, she dressed more modestly.

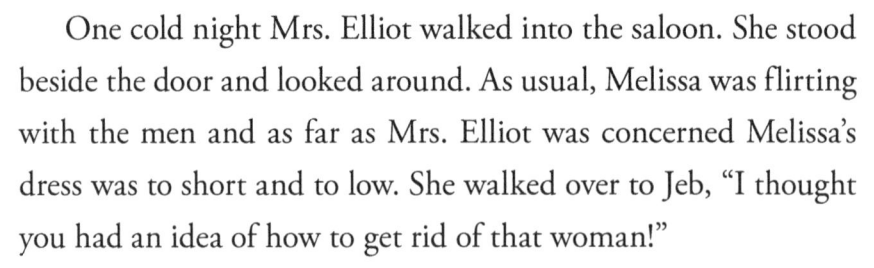

One cold night Mrs. Elliot walked into the saloon. She stood beside the door and looked around. As usual, Melissa was flirting with the men and as far as Mrs. Elliot was concerned Melissa's dress was to short and to low. She walked over to Jeb, "I thought you had an idea of how to get rid of that woman!"

"The plan is in progress, you just can't see it." Jeb put his arm around Mrs. Elliot. "I want to get rid of her as much as you girls. Every day I see her I am reminded of San Francisco. Believe me; I want to get rid of her."

Mrs. Elliot took off her coat and handed it to Jeb. She walked over to a table and took their order. She walked back to the kitchen, laid her tray on the bar, and waited. Jeb, carrying her coat walked over to her. "How did things go at the bank today?"

"A lot of gold and silver came in again," she said looking into his blue eyes. "Are you making a deposit tomorrow?"

"Planning a robbery are you?" Jeb asked grinning at her.

"No, of course not," she said softly. "You have been good to me and I appreciate it. I just wished you did not have me working so many hours."

"There are some people worth giving a second chance and some are not."

"Why me and not Mr. Langsford?"

"Mr. Langsford could not tell the truth if he had to," Jeb said as he looked out over the saloon. "You told me up front about your husband."

"When do you think I will hear from Mr. Langsford?" She ask.

"I doubt if you do," Jeb said looking away from her. "You know the old saying; Absence makes the heart grow fonder for someone else. I wouldn't worry about it, he wasn't worth it."

"You're certainly helpful!" She spat.

"I try to be," Jeb said as he patted her hand. "But think about it. You're here, broke; he is California with a few thousand dollars."

"I miss him, but not as much as I used to," Mrs. Elliot said sadly. "It would be nice to have a man."

Jeb looked at Mrs. Elliot with questions written on his face. "You women are strange. After Melissa, it was ten years before I let a woman near me. That woman was Sharon. Mr. Langsford has been gone only three months and you're crying already."

Mrs. Elliot looked at Melissa then at Jeb. "Can I work in the kitchen? I know I'll not make as much money, but I hate that woman."

"Yeah," Jeb said quietly. "She dresses to make money, why don't you?"

Mrs. Elliot looked at Jeb with daggers in her eyes. "I am thirty five years old and am not a hussy."

"When a fella is drunk or getting drunk age or looks don't matter," Jeb said laughing. "You did it with Mr. Langsford, why not any miner that comes along?"

Mrs. Elliot slapped Jeb as hard as she could. "I may have been a whore but that does not mean I am one now!" She whispered hatefully.

Jeb rubbed his face. "Your right," he said slowly.

Sharon had heard the slap and walked over to Jeb. "Did you deserve it?"

Jeb nodded. "She is jealous Melissa is making more money by spending the nights with a miner or two, she could do the same. What's the big deal, one guy or two guys?"

"Jeb," Sharon whispered tenderly. "Look at me."

Jeb turned to look at Sharon. He smiled when he saw her angry face. Suddenly she slapped him. "Mrs. Elliot is trying to be a decent lady. Then you stick her working with the likes of Melissa. You need to be shot!" Sharon stormed out of the kitchen.

"What's the matter," Sandy asked as Sharon walked passed her and pushed her out of the way.

When Sharon reached the back door, she stopped and turned to face Sandy. "That husband of mine is no better than Mr. Elliot. He's trying to get Mrs. Elliot to spend nights with the miners."

Sandy hurried over to Jeb. "Is it true what Sharon said about what you told Mrs. Elliot?"

"Yes, but…."

Sandy slapped Jeb and started to hit him again. Jeb grabbed her arm. "All right, already, I get the message. Mrs. Elliot get back here right now!"

Mrs. Elliot hurried back to where Jeb and Sandy were standing. Sharon was walking up to Jeb.

"Yes, Mr. Pearson," Mrs. Elliot purred as she stopped in front of him.

"I apologize for saying what I said about you and the miners. If you do not want to work here any longer, it will be okay, but we do need your help. These winter months can be brutal as you know."

"Thank you, Mr. Pearson," Mrs. Elliot said slyly. "You can be a nice person after all."

Sharon grasped Jeb's hand. He turned to her and she smiled and whispered in his ear.

"We'll be back in a while," Jeb said happily as he and Sharon started for the back door.

"Where are you going on a snowy day like today? Mrs. Elliot asked.

"Sharon is keeping her promise," Jeb said smiling happily.

"Jeb Pearson, why do you have to be such a scoundrel?" Sharon asked as Jeb opened the door.

"They would have figured it out anyway," he said closing the door.

CHAPTER 17

After a while, Sharon and Jeb returned to the saloon. Jeb went to the ice chest and poured himself a glass of milk. He sat down at a table in the kitchen. Melissa came into the kitchen all bouncy and happy.

"Jeb, there's a man out here to see you," Melissa said as she bent over so Jeb could see more of her breasts.

"Who is it?" he asked getting up from the table.

"How should I know?" She said turning toward the saloon and strutting out of the kitchen.

"When are you going to get rid of that woman?" Sharon hissed.

"I'm working on it," he said walking toward the door to the saloon. "Be patient."

"I am running out of patience," Sharon hissed hatefully.

"There will never be anything between me and that witch," Jeb said happily. "I married you because of who you are, not what you have. Anyone who marries her will have a couple of nice things but that is all. She ain't got no brains."

Sandy turned to Sharon. "He is being honest with you."

"Sometimes I wonder," Sharon, hissed still angry with Melissa.

Mrs. Elliot sat down in a chair and began fixing herself a sandwich. "I have seen him look at Melissa with contempt. I have never seen him look at her the way he looks at you. I would love to have a man look at me the way he does you."

Sandy sat down at the table and began fixing herself a sandwich. "This winter no one is going anywhere, so it may take him till spring to get rid of her. It's like Mrs. Elliot said, 'he looks at you like he looks at no other woman.' You're lucky Sharon, be patient. How many of Jeb's ideas have failed?"

Sharon sat down at the table and began fixing herself a sandwich. "None that I can think of. But there is always the first time and I guess that is what scares me."

Jeb walked out into the saloon. A man wearing a well-made suit walked up to him and offered his hand for a handshake. "I am Mr. Harry Reynolds. I am with the Melton Investment Company. I am looking for Mr. Langsford. He is behind in his payments and has disappeared."

"Oh," Jeb said surprised. "What do you mean disappeared?"

"I don't know that he has disappeared, the company has not heard from him for over three months. Was he married or do you know?"

Yes, he was. In fact, his wife works for me. She is a cook."

"May I meet her?" He ask.

"Of course," Jeb said leading the man to his office, "Make yourself comfortable, I'll be right back." Jeb hurried to the kitchen. He took Mrs. Elliot by the arm and led her to a corner. "From now on you're Mrs. Langsford. I just found out why he told you someday you and him would be rich. You tell him the truth except that you and Mr. Langsford were secretly married. You will gladly show him the papers tomorrow."

"But that's dishonest."

"I thought you wanted to go back to California?"

"I do," Mrs. Elliot said nervously.

"Here's your chance, now do it."

Mrs. Elliot left the kitchen and walked to the office.

Jeb turned to Sharon and Sandy. "I don't care how you do it, get Melissa drunk and passed out. She does not know anything and I want her out of the picture."

"I have some lithium," Sandy said happily. "It used to put me out for hours."

"How did you take it?" Jeb ask.

"With some whiskey," Sandy said softly.

"Get Melissa out of the picture. Lie to her, or whatever you have to do to get her out."

Jeb left the kitchen and went to the office.

Melissa stormed into the kitchen. "Where did Mrs. Elliot go? It's crowded out there and I need help."

"Jeb made a new drink and we have all tried it," Sandy said slowly as she offered the glass to Melissa. "Sit down and enjoy it."

"It's pretty good," Sharon said happily. "It put me in the mood for Jeb."

"As tired as I am getting I need something to put me in the mood." Melissa sat down and looked suspiciously at the two girls. She did not like the way they were looking at her. She drank the drink in one swallow. "What's in it?" Melissa said as she put the glass down.

"You would have to ask Jeb," Sandy said happily. "He is talking about selling it in the saloon."

Melissa started to stand up, and as she did so she began to weave and she sat down again. She shook her head several times. "What did you do to me?"

"Nothing," Sandy said seriously. "If it's bothering you this way it might affect other people the same way and that's not good."

Melissa fell to the floor, asleep. Sandy and Sharon shook hands knowing Melissa was going to be out for quite a while.

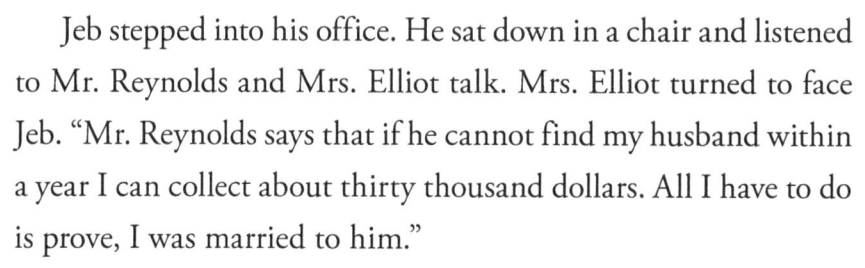

Jeb stepped into his office. He sat down in a chair and listened to Mr. Reynolds and Mrs. Elliot talk. Mrs. Elliot turned to face Jeb. "Mr. Reynolds says that if he cannot find my husband within a year I can collect about thirty thousand dollars. All I have to do is prove, I was married to him."

"If you're like everyone else you keep your records at the courthouse?"

"Of course, Mrs. Elliot replied. "That's the safest place outside the bank."

"Mr. Reynolds," Jeb said standing up. "I don't know how you got here in this weather but I can guarantee you're not going anywhere now until spring."

"I came in by dogsled and will going back the same way."

"Good," Jeb said happily. "I'll have the cooks fix you a big steak and you can have any one of the girls you want to join you."

"I would be pleased to have Mrs. Langsford join me."

"Very good," Jeb said standing up. "The table back by the window is nice, I'll bring you a drink and as soon as the steaks are ready I will bring them out to you." Jeb hurried to the kitchen. He smiled when he saw Melissa on the floor asleep. "That stuff works. "Fix another one, this time it's for Mr. Reynolds."

"What's going on?" Sharon asked impatiently.

"When Mrs. Elliot told me who he was and what she could get. I had an idea."

Sharon covered her face with her hands. "Not another one?"

"This one will make Mrs. Elliot fairly wealthy."

"Really, and what about us?" Sharon asked.

"You're already rich and you know it,"

"I know," Sharon said sadly. "Married to a man rich in ideas."

"It could be worse," Jeb said in his defense.

"How?" Sharon asked.

"I don't know." He answered.

Sandy handed Jeb the two drinks. "The one on the right is for Mrs. Elliot and the one on the left is for what's his name. As you walk toward them, the drinks are on the tray the way they are supposed to be given to them.

"Don't you trust me?" He ask.

"No," the ladies answered in unison.

Jeb rolled his eyes back in his head and started into the saloon.

After the first drink, Mr. Reynolds began getting sleepy. Jeb put the steak on the table in front of him. "I think you traveled too far in the cold weather," Jeb said calmly. "I did it once and slept for quite a while."

"Perhaps so," Mr. Reynolds said. "Perhaps I'd better go to my room at the hotel."

Jeb winked at Mrs. Elliot. "Go with Mr. Reynolds and make sure he gets tucked in tight."

Mrs. Elliot looked at Jeb with contempt.

"It's okay, Mrs. Langsford," Jeb said quietly. "I promise."

Mr. Reynolds stood to his feet and weaved a bit. "Finish this," Jeb said, handing the drink to Mr. Reynolds. "No sense letting a good drink go to waste."

Mrs. Elliot smiled because she knew Jeb had done something. Jeb helped Mr. Reynolds out the door to the hotel and Jeb had to carry him to his hotel room. He took off all his clothes except his long johns. He and Mrs. Elliot went back to the saloon.

When they entered the saloon, Mrs. Elliot went to the kitchen. She was surprised to see Melissa propped up in a corner sound asleep.

"What is going on?" she asked puzzled by Melissa sleeping and Mr. Reynolds being put to sleep.

"We will never tell," Sandy said proudly. "Melissa will not be a problem for a while and Mr. Reynolds will be out for who knows how long or why."

Jeb stepped into the kitchen. "Mrs. Elliot, bundle up, you're going with me. Whatever you do, do not ask any questions."

"Jeb!" Sharon cried desperately. "What is going on?"

"Trust me," Jeb said as he put on his coat and hat. He gave Sharon a peck on the cheek. "I love you, remember that!"

CHAPTER 18

Jeb led Mrs. Elliot to the courthouse. He went around to the back and beat on the door. Finally, Mr. Perkins answered it. "What is it Jeb, I am trying to sleep."

"Look old man, how would you like to make a thousand dollars?"

"That would nice, but how can I do that?"

Jeb grabbed Mrs. Elliot by the arm and pushed her into the apartment. "I need a marriage license and divorce papers. I also need some papers with Mr. Langsford and Mr. Elliot's signatures."

"What for?" Mr. Perkins ask.

"So you can make a thousand dollars. Just get me two sets of each leave me and this lady alone and you will have a thousand dollars as soon as Mr. Reynolds leaves town."

Mr. Perkins shrugged his shoulders and led them through the apartment to the records division of the courthouse. He obtained the papers Jeb had requested. "What was the name of the preacher that died about five years ago?" Jeb ask.

"Uh, uh Wesley Hardin," Mr. Perkins said quietly.

"Have you got a copy of his signature?" Jeb ask.

Mr. Perkins obtained a copy of the preacher's signature and gave it to Jeb.

"What about Judge Fields?" Jeb ask.

"Jeb, you're up to no good, I can feel it," Mr. Perkins said slowly.

"I am going to leave all these papers on this desk," Jeb said looking at Mr. Perkins. "You file them properly and do as you're told and I'll add another five hundred."

Mrs. Elliot smiled as she realized what Jeb was going to attempt. "I'll throw in a thousand if you are convincing enough."

"Ba, ba ba, that's two thousand five hundred dollars," Mr. Perkins panted.

"For keeping your mouth shut." Jeb said.

"Goodnight," Mr. Perkins said as he left the room.

Jeb began filling out the papers and studying the handwriting of each man whose signature was going to be forged. "While I am writing, please don't say anything."

Jeb filled out the papers accordingly and handed them to Mrs. Elliot and she signed them as well.

"Well," Jeb said when they were finished. How does it feel to be divorced from Mr. Elliot and married to Mr. Langsford?"

"Where did you learn to do almost perfect copies of a man's signature?"

"Law school!" Jeb answered.

"Law school?" Mrs. Elliot asked in an astonished voice.

"Yep, I figured it would do me some good one day," Jeb said chuckling. "I transferred five thousand from a bankers account to mine and he could not argue with the signature."

"Jeb, I can't believe…." She said.

"Look, I told you there are people worth giving a second chance. It's here, take it." He answered.

Later that night Jeb crawled into bed next to Sharon. "Where have you been?" She asked as she woke up.

"Making money," Jeb said quietly. "For Mrs. Elliott."

"Jeb," Sharon said sitting up. "Between the saloon and the gold mining, we have more than enough money to…"

"If we have kids they cost money!" Jeb whispered.

"What did you and Mrs. Elliot do?" Sharon asked.

"I got her divorced from Mr. Elliot and married to Mr. Langsford."

"Mr. Elliot is dead and Mr. Langsford is in California," Sharon said confused by Jeb's answer.

"Sharon, go back to sleep or keep your promise." He said.

"Which do you want me to do?" She asked.

"I want you to go to sleep and keep your promise in the morning." Jeb said smiling.

The next morning Melissa walked into the kitchen. She looked at Sandy. "What was that drink you gave me?"

"I don't know," Sandy said softly. "Jeb made it."

"I sure slept good," Melissa said as she sat down at the table. "I don't remember going to bed, but I woke up in bed by myself."

"That's unusual," Sandy said quietly.

"But I slept well. Do you think Jeb would fix me another one tonight? I feel rested and if I could have another night's sleep like I had last night….."

"It's about time you got here," Jeb said as he walked into the kitchen.

"Jeb, can you fix me another drink like you did last night, I slept so well and I feel rested."

"How about I fix you one now, I need you here tonight."

Melissa shook her head. "How about when I get off work?"

"Alright," Jeb said softly. "Mrs. Elliot found a fella last night and I don't want you interfering."

"How did she do that?" She old," Melissa argued.

"It happened, so I suggest you let them be." Jeb said with anger.

Sandy handed Melissa a drink. "This will keep your mind off your loneliness," Sandy said as she looked at Jeb and nodded. A few minutes later Jeb put Melissa over his shoulder and carried her back to her room.

Jeb was coming out of the kitchen when Mr. Reynolds and Mrs. Elliot entered the saloon.

"Good morning Jeb," Mrs. Elliot said happily.

"Are we ready to go to the courthouse?"

The three walked in the blinding snowstorm to the courthouse. Mr. Perkins smiled when he saw them. "What can I do for you?"

"I would like to show this man my divorce papers from Mr. Elliot and my marriage license to Mr. Langsford." Mrs. Elliot said.

Mr. Perkins obtained the papers and handed them to Mr. Reynolds. He looked them over carefully. The paper appears old and the ink fresh.

"That happens a lot," Mr. Perkins said seriously. "Here is Jeb's marriage license and you can see it is the same way."

"Everything looks in order. I will authorize the transfer from Mr. to Mrs." Mr. Reynolds said smiling.

"Thank you," Mrs. Elliot said as she smiled at Jeb.

"Thank you, Mr. Pearson," Mr. Reynolds said as he shook his hand.

"Your welcome." Jeb said smiling.

The three walked back to the saloon. Mr. Reynolds sat at a table and ordered lunch from Sandy. Mrs. Elliot went to the kitchen. Jeb called George into his office.

George sat in a chair. Jeb sat behind his desk.

"Are you good with a dogsled?" Jeb asked.

"Sure, nothing to it. I've been out in the worst of weather with a team."

"Did you see the man I came into the saloon with?"

"Yeah," George said indifferently. "That city dude?"

"It is extremely important you get him and Mr. Elliot to Wastach."

"Can I have a free night with Melissa?" George asked.

Just tell her I said, "She was free for tonight."

That night Melissa stormed into Jeb's office. "What do you mean I'm free to George? I hate him."

"Are you forgetting who you work for?" Jeb asked.

"No, I haven't forgot who I work for," Melissa said softly.

"Aren't you enjoying your free food and drinks and all the men you want?"

"Yes, but him!"

"It won't be so bad," Jeb said laughing. "Just think it could be me instead of him."

Melissa narrowed her eyes in hatred as she looked at Jeb. "Someday I am going to kill you."

CHAPTER 19

THE SNOWMELT HAD BEGUN WHEN a huge man entered the saloon. He looked around for a few minutes. "Gimmie a bottle!" He demanded.

"Sorry," Melissa said smiling at him. "We can only serve drinks a glass at a time."

"Where's the owner of this mangy place," he yelled.

Jeb came out of the kitchen. "I'm right here,' he said walking over to the man. "What do you need?"

"I need a bottle, not a glass!" He roared.

Jeb took a deep sigh. "Can we go to my office and discuss this?"

"Yeah I guess so," the man growled.

"Melissa, bring a bottle of the best whiskey to the office, and hurry."

The man and Jeb went into the office and sat down. A few minutes later Melissa came into the office with a bottle of whiskey and two glasses. She smiled at the big man as she leaned forward, revealing her breast for him to see, as she poured him a glass of whiskey.

"Thank you Melissa," Jeb said as she poured him his glass. Melissa left the office and closed the door. "How are you Bear?"

"Great, how's Jeb?" He said looking back at the door. "Where did you find her? She has got a great pair."

"I know," Jeb said softly. "She's the one I told you about that pretended to get shot and had me put in jail."

"Yeah I remember you telling me about that," Bear replied.

"How would you like to have her?" Jeb ask.

"That would be great!" Bear said as the excitement entered his voice.

"No, I mean to take with you back to your camp and keep her there." He said.

"For how long?" Bear ask.

"Until you got tired of her, then you could feed her to the wolves."

Bear looked at Jeb suspiciously. "What's going on?"

"She's causing problems here at the saloon between my wife and I!" Jeb said in anger.

"So you figure a guy like me who only goes into town for the winter needs a woman year round!" Bear said laughing.

"Well, yeah," Jeb said slowly.

Bear rubbed his beard slowly as he looked at Jeb. "You saved my life once, so I owe you. But how did you end up getting married? You were single for a long time."

Jeb quickly told the story of the adventure he and Sharon had out maneuvering Mr. Elliot and the final gunfight and obtaining the saloon.

"So now you're happy?" Bear ask.

Jeb nodded. "She promised me whenever I wanted it I could have it and she has kept that promise and yes, I am happy with her."

"Can I meet her?" Bear ask.

Jeb walked over to the door, he opened it and looked out over the saloon. "Melissa, come here for a minute!"

Melissa hurried to the office. "What do you want, I'm busy!"

"This gentleman wants another shot of whiskey and wanted you to pour it for him."

Melissa smiled as she poured the whiskey. Bear smiled as she leaned over to fill his glass.

"Tell Sharon I want her in the office now!" Jeb demanded.

"Of course," Melissa snapped hatefully. She smiled at Bear. "If you finish that one real quick I'll pour you another one."

Bear swallowed the drink in one swallow. His smile was huge as Melissa poured him another drink. Melissa left the office and hurried to the kitchen. A few minutes later Sharon entered the office.

"Sharon, this is Bear. He is the man whose life I saved up in the mountains a few years back."

"I'm glad to meet you," Sharon said happily. "Jeb certainly made a difference in how my life was going. I must get back to the kitchen."

"Nice!" Bear said after Sharon left the office.

"What did you think of the other one?" Jeb asked his voice filled with curiosity.

"She'd be nice to have. How much are you going to pay me to take her?" Bear ask.

"Pay you, I thought you would do an old friend a favor." Jeb said smiling.

"It's gonna cost to feed her. She don't look like she would be a good worker!" Bear said as thoughts of Melissa filled his mind and he looked toward the office door.

"But think of those….." Jeb said smiling.

"Alright, I'll take her, but what if she don't want to go?" Bear ask.

"She will have no choice." Jeb said smiling.

Bear looked at Jeb. "What do you mean no choice?"

"I'll give her some stuff that will make her sleep and when she wakes up she will be at your cabin or on the way." Jeb said seriously.

"Ain't this slightly against the law?" Bear ask.

"Not if no one hears from her again." Jeb said with a wicked grin.

"Yeah, Bear said as he was thinking. I only go into town for the winter by dogsled and she would have to stay at the cabin so who is she going to tell?

Precisely, Jeb said as a huge smile crossed his face.

"When?" Bear ask.

We'll wake her early in the morning and go from there, Jeb said standing up. Be at the back door at 6:00 am.

That night Jeb pulled a dirty trick on Sharon, Sandy and Mrs. Elliot. He poured some drugs in each one of their drinks they had after work. Each one of them made it to their rooms and slept soundly.

Just before sunrise, Jeb was in Melissa's room waking her up. Come on Melissa, he urged. Sharon is sick and you need to fix breakfast. Melissa dressed and walked slowly down the stairs. When she entered the kitchen, Bear and Jeb were having a cup of coffee. Sit down and have a cup, Jeb said happily. You can talk to Bear while I check on Sharon.

Jeb hurried to Melissa's room and began putting her dresses and shoes into some cloth bags. When he arrived back at the kitchen Bear was coming in from outside.

She is sound asleep and is tucked away safely. There are plenty of blankets around her feet and body so she won't get cold. The canvas ought to protect her from the wind.

"Here are her dresses, put them where they will be added protection from the cold.

"Thanks", Bear said happily.

"Enjoy the view." Jeb said.

Bear smiled happily. "I plan to do more than that!"

Jeb stood at the door until the dogsled was out of sight. He walked back into the kitchen and poured out all the coffee. He went back up to his room, undressed and crawled in bed with Sharon. He decided to stay there until she woke up.

Bear made his way across the hills and small mountains to his shack. He built a fire in the stove, then carried Melissa into the cabin and laid her on the bed. He tied her wrists and feet to the four corners of the bed.

Bear was outside feeding the dogs when he heard Melissa screaming. He finished feeding the dogs and walked calmly into the cabin. "Where am I?" She screamed, her voice filled with hate. "Untie me this minute!"

Bear sat down on the edge of the bed. "You're at my cabin. And I can't untie you until you understand a few things."

"Like what?" She hissed hatefully.

"I needed a housekeeper and a cook," Bear said running his hand along her throat and down toward her breasts.

"Get your hands off me," Melissa screamed at the top of her voice. "I'll kill you and Jeb when I get the chance." Bear got up and took one of Melissa's scarves out of the bag. He sat back on the edge of the bed. "You and Jeb double-crossed me and I'll get even." Bear clutched her throat forcing her to open her mouth and he stuffed the scarf in it.

"I needed a housekeeper, a cook and someone to spend time with. Jeb thought you were ideal. I don't have a horse, but I do have a dog team. I go into town after first snow and don't come back until the spring melt begins. It is a one-day journey to town. If you try to walk it, you will get lost. The grizzly bears, and wolves are always looking for food. You have a choice stay here or die. I had a bear tear up one of my dogs one year. Believe me you want to stay here."

Bear walked outside to check on his dogs leaving Melissa struggling to get free. Melissa pulled and tugged and the ropes that bound her. She tried to spew out the scarf, but it began going deeper into her throat. Bear came into the cabin and walked over to the stove. He heard Melissa choking and pulled the scarf out of her mouth. "I hate you," she screamed. Bear stretched the scarf its full length. He put it around Melissa's head from the back and tied it so the tie was in her mouth. He sat down on the edge of the bed. "I really don't like doing this to you, but you have to understand, if you kill me you will either freeze or starve to death. Then again, you can be the good whore you were in Fairbanks. Your choice!"

CHAPTER 20

MELISSA REMAINED TIED TO THE bed for almost a week. Her hands were tied behind her back and she was blind folded and taken outside for her bodily functions. She slowly began to realize she was in a helpless situation. The summer passed with Bear doing all the work and Melissa sitting in a corner pouting.

The first snow fell and bear went to town leaving Melissa at the cabin. Melissa put wood on the fire and some of it burned and some of it did not. Over the course of the day, she put the fire out and there were only burning embers below the wood. Too often, when the wood started burning she moved the wood and the fire on the wood would go out.

Late in the afternoon, she began to realize she was colder than she had been all day. She bundled up in some caribou skins to stay warm. She finally curled up on the bed and huddled in a ball to stay warm. When Bear arrived back at the cabin, he saw a bundle of furs on the bed. "Melissa," he yelled.

"I'm in bed," she whispered. "I'm so cold."

Bear pulled back the skins to look at her. "I'm so cold, please help me!" She said as her voice quivered from the cold.

Bear uncovered her legs and began rubbing them. "God, you're cold," he said covering up her legs. He went over to the stove and began building a fire. He put a pan of water on the stove. He sat back on the edge of the bed and had Melissa roll over on her stomach. He began rubbing her back. He laid his head on her back and held her tight. "Don't leave me, Melissa, please don't leave me."

"I'm so cold," Melissa groaned.

"I know," Bear said as he covered her up. He poured the water into a cup and gave it to her to drink.

"This water is hot!" she screamed.

"This water is barely warm." He said.

"It's hot," Melissa screamed.

"Good you're getting better," he said taking off his coat and laying it over Melissa.

Bear threw more wood on the fire, took off his clothes down to his red long Johns, and crawled under the blankets with Melissa.

"You feel so hot to me," Melissa whispered.

"Maybe my body will help warm up your body," Bear said as he kissed Melissa on the forehead. Melissa moved closer to him as she felt the warmth of his body.

"Why did you ask me not to leave you? Melissa whispered.

"It's been nice to have you here, even if you won't talk to me. I am kinda fond of you." Bear said as he kissed her on the forehead.

"This ain't the best place to have a wife. I ain't rich like Jeb, but its home and nobody bothers me."

Melissa put her arms around Bear. "I have given you nothing but trouble. I don't understand why you feed me when I do so little. I cook and help you just to have something to do."

"Wouldn't it be better if we worked as a team?" Bear asked.

"You won't take me out of here?"

"No, I would kill you before I would let you leave me," Bear whispered.

"Do you hate me that much?" Melissa said as she took her arms from around him.

"I don't hate you, but I don't love you either," Bear said as he rubbed her stomach.

"I thought you would be someone to talk to, but you're not even that. All you do is consume food and do as little as possible."

"What else am I supposed to do?" Melissa asked bitterly as she turned away from facing him. "You bring me wherever I am, against my will and then expect anything you want and for me to work. I don't like rats."

"How do you think Jeb felt when you had him put in jail on false charges of getting shot?"

"I'll kill both of you if I get the chance," Melissa hissed in hate.

"I see you don't even appreciate my saving your life," Bear said hatefully. He threw back the blankets and skins, grabbed Melissa by the hair, and dragged her toward the door.

"What are you doing?" she screamed.

"Getting rid of you, town is that way," Bear yelled pointing to the east."

"But it's dark, I'll never make it in these clothes."

"Tough," Bear yelled as he struggled to open the door. He twisted Melissa's arm behind her back pushed her out the door and shut it.

Melissa beat on the door begging to be let back in. "Please, I'm cold, Bear, please let me in." She realized the door was not going to be opened and she let her body slide down the wall until she was sitting on the ground.

Bear opened the door, grabbed her by the hair, and pulled her inside. Melissa tried to put her arms around him. "Thank you, Bear, please let me give you a kiss."

Bear shoved Melissa against the wall. She hit it hard and fell to the floor with the wind knocked out of her. She began crawling for the bed. "Please, let me get under the blankets to get warm. Please!" She cried desperately.

Melissa crawled onto the bed and covered up. She lay shivering. This time Bear did not get in bed with her. He dressed and stoked the fire.

"Jeb was right," Bear yelled. "You do not appreciate anything anyone does for you. I'd let you go, just to get rid of you, but I know you'd try to kill Jeb."

"No I won't," she said uncovering her face. "Please put me on the boat to California."

"You get to California and you will go running to the officials and have him put back in jail. Not on your life, you stupid bitch.

Jeb saved my life once, I owe him, and keeping you up here is paying him back. But you make me wonder if it is worth it. He is right about one thing - your trash."

Melissa covered her head with the blankets. Bear uncovered her head. She looked up at him through her tears. "No one has ever called me that before. He is right I faked a gunshot wound; put him in jail so some building projects could go forward. I helped plan his jailbreak and waited a few years before coming to look for him. Then Joshua is killed. It's a different miner every night."

Bear sat down next to her. "We could be happy if you would let us."

"You don't mean that!" She screamed.

"Yes I do," Bear said as he stroked her hair. "When I saw the size of those I wanted you, still do, but now for a different reason."

Melissa toyed with his hand as he stroked her cheek. "That's all men ever wanted me for, was my size, why should you be different?"

"We ain't leaving here until the second snow. What do you say we work on it?"

Melissa pushed his hand away from her and huddled under the covers. "It will not do any good," she whispered. "I know why you wanted me."

"You mean you're not even willing to try?" Bear asked with disappointment in his voice.

"I've been a whore all my life," Melissa said as the tears began to flow. "How do you expect me to change? Jeb gave me to you because he doesn't want me around.

"Did you ever think why he did not want you around?" He ask.

Melissa looked at Bear strangely. "No," she whispered. "I guess it was because I was always showing my breasts to him and causing trouble between him and Sharon."

"Why don't you try doing what you think might work?"

The rest of the summer, the couple worked on breaking the bad rock from around the gold. During the fall, a huge landslide almost took out the cabin. They were looking at the damage to the mountain when they saw some glittering gold rocks. Bear and Melissa had struck it rich.

CHAPTER 21

$\mathcal{F}$IVE YEARS LATER MELISSA AND Bear went into Fairbanks. The dogsled had been left at a cabin and Bear was trying to sell his dogs. Melissa walked into the saloon. Sharon immediately recognized her. She walked over to her as anger flushed through her body. "I suppose you want to cause trouble?"

"No," Melissa said softly. "But I do want to see Jeb and thank him for what he did for me?"

"What did he do?" Sharon asked with confusion in her voice. "I knew you disappeared, but no one told me where you went."

"Jeb double-crossed me, like I did him," Melissa said sadly. "Jeb went to jail. Jeb gave me to Bear and he took me way back in the mountains. He took me a while to get used to life back there. We spent the winters in a small town and the summers at the mine. Four years ago, a landslide almost took out our cabin. There was more gold waiting to be picked up than you can imagine. Bear and I are going back to California and live quietly."

Jeb entered the saloon followed by Bear. "I heard the good news Melissa," Jeb said as he took a revolver out of his coat. "I can't let you go back to California."

Bear grabbed Jeb's arm. "You shoot Melissa and I will kill you," he said squeezing Jeb's arm.

Jeb's face winched in pain. "What am I supposed to do let her go to the police like she wants to do?"

Melissa walked over to Jeb. "I am not going to the cops. Once we get on that ship and we get to California Bear and I are going somewhere where it is warm all year to live. When you gave me to Bear, you did the greatest favor a man could ever do for me. Bear and I are in love with one another. I know what it is to work together – as a team. When we get on the ship, you will never hear from me again. I am going to leave you alone and I want you to leave me alone."

Jeb turned to Bear. "Are you sure this is the Melissa I gave to you?"

"Yep, Bear said happily. "She and I had long talks and many a night of loving one another and she's changed and so have I. We probably won't stay in California very long."

"Long enough to tell the police where I am!"

"No, Jeb," Melissa said sadly. "I know you and Sharon are happy. You deserve that. I don't deserve it, but Bear and I are happy."

"I wish I could believe you," Jeb said slowly.

Melissa began unbuttoning her coat. "Remember, the dresses I used to wear?" She took off her coat.

"What's a dress got to do with it? Jeb asked.

"Bear told me he didn't like me showing off to every man. After we were married, I began to dress more like Sharon and Mrs. Elliot. Bear likes it too."

"I must say you do look nicer than in the past," Jeb said shaking his head. "I guess, I will trust you," he said softly. "I want you out of my saloon, never to come back."

"I understand," Melissa said softly as she put on her coat. Thank you for giving me to Bear."

"Your welcome."

Late that night Jeb slipped out of the saloon. He went to the boat dock. He hurried up to the captain's quarters.

"Hello Jeb, who this time?"

"You remember Melissa?" He ask.

"How could one forget her I mean she was …?" The captain ask.

"She said she is going by boat to California. I know she will be going to the police. Can you…?"

"Let me see if she is on the manifest!" The captain looked over the list. "There is not a Melissa even listed here."

"There has to be she said she was going to be on the boat and she emphasized that fact," Jeb said.

"Look for yourself," The captain said.

Jeb looked over the passenger list. "She nor Bear are on the list. There are no married couples going back to California. She lied to me again," Jeb said disgusted.

"You know what I think Jeb!" The captain said softly. "I think Melissa and Bear came to town to make you worry and have gone back to their mine."

"If you see her?" Jeb ask.

"I will take care of her," the captain said softly. "You can count on it."

Jeb went back to the saloon. When he entered it, he saw Sharon waiting by the bar. "Where have you been?" She asked.

"Looking for Bear, I wanted to say good bye to him."

"What about Melissa?"

"I don't care about Melissa. I never missed her these past five years and I doubt if I will miss her for the next ten. You are the only women in my life Sharon. You have been from the day we met."

"I'm glad," Sharon whispered in his ear. "Do you want me to keep my promise?"

"Let's go," Jeb said happily.

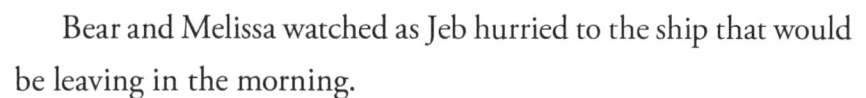

Bear and Melissa watched as Jeb hurried to the ship that would be leaving in the morning.

Melissa looked at Bear. "We cannot take the ship. The captain is related to Jeb and he is no doubt planning to have the captain throw me overboard."

"The only other way out of here is by horseback, buggy, or dogsled," Bear said softly. "If there was another ship, but there isn't. I do not want to take the chance of being on that ship and having to fight the crew to save you. Do you want to try a buggy?" Bear said softly.

Melissa nodded. "When he finds out we are not on that ship it is going to drive him crazy wondering where I am. Let us take the buggy. You and I are good enough shots we can handle about any situation."

The couple hurried to the mercantile store and purchased more blankets and coats. They hurried to the stable and purchased a horse and buggy. They began their journey across the wilderness to Washington.

As promised, Melissa never talked to the police. She sent a letter to Jeb stating that she and Bear were living down the street from a policeman and she often felt tempted to talk to him. Melissa never told Jeb, she and Bear remained in California for the winter, and then moved to Apache Junction, Arizona.

When Jeb received the letter, he read it and tore it up in anger knowing he should not have trusted Melissa. Thereafter, he remained out of sight for two or three days each time the boat docked.